CAPTAIN DEATH

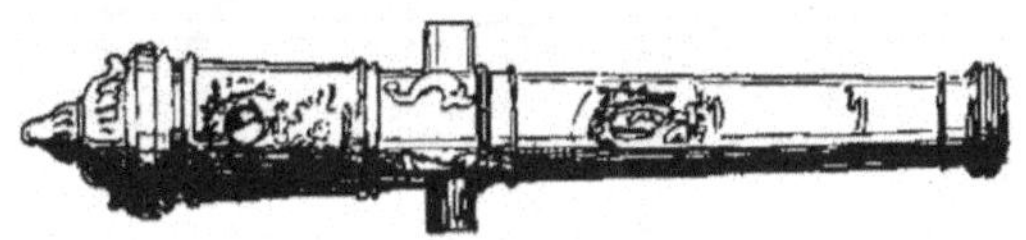

Jürgen Vsych

(pronounced Yurgen VY-zick)

Wroughten Books

Philadelphia

TheCaptainDeath.com

For you

Captain
Death
Jurgen
Wroughten Books
Not the same old rot

Boston Tea Party, 16 December 1773

CHAPTERS

I	Thomas Jefferson Hates Clancy	1
II	Blackbeard's Host	9
III	Clancy is Hung…or Hanged	16
IV	Naider's Raiders	25
V	The King's Arms	39
VI	Laughingstock of the Seven Seas	43
VII	Clancy Gets Himself to a Nunnery	51
VIII	Clancy Beats Up a Priest	57
IX	Aunt Anne Bonny	63
X	George Washington's Musical Glasses	71
XI	In Scotland with Benjamin Franklin and David Hume	85
XII	To Philadelphia with Thomas Pain(e)	101
XIII	The Chocolate Pirate	112
XIV	John Adams Flips His Wig	119
XV	Clancy of Culloden	126
XVI	Knocking Common Sense into Thomas Paine	138
XVII	Paul Revere's Teapot	147
XVIII	George Washington's Biggest Mistake	157
XIX	Kiss a Pirate	167
XX	The Terrible II	174
XXI	Captain Death	181

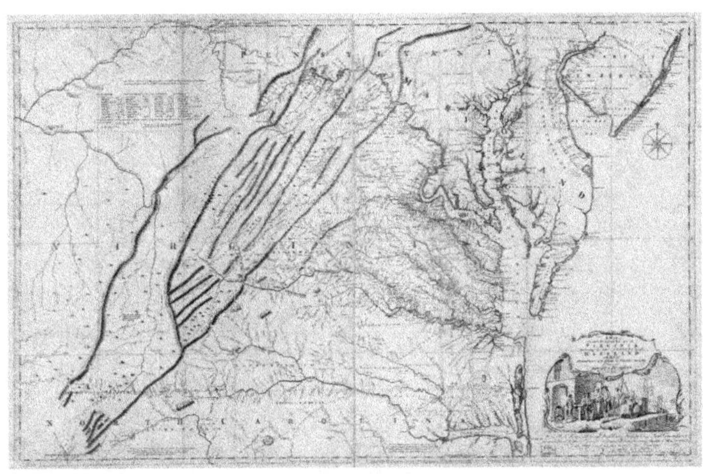

I
THOMAS JEFFERSON HATES CLANCY

June 2, 1774

Clancy Redbeard drove Thomas Jefferson crazy. Clancy had the education, manners, and charm to marry a fine lady – a rich widow, perhaps, as Jefferson had – but he married a hog farmer's shrewish daughter and had sunk to this: busking in front of the King's Arms Tavern, playing musical glasses.

And Clancy had sat at the feet of Virginia's Royal Governor when he was but four years old! Jefferson had to wait until he was a student of lawyer George Wythe (and was only invited because the governor needed a violinist after Patrick Henry quit his chamber ensemble). But Clancy was a Redbeard, and thus given free rein of the palace and leave to ask any upstart question that suited the four-year-old son of a pirate. With those lethal smiles, the Redbeards could get away with murder – and had. Clancy could ask, *where is the silver kept? And where might the governor store his secret supply of gunpowder?* and the governor would have shown him! He would have told Clancy the exact number of guns, swords, and cannon! Wars were lost over such indiscreet drunken blathering. And where did all these privileges and advantages lead Clancy? To standing in the gutter, playing Händel's *Water Music* on musical glasses…!

Jefferson took a deep breath, and told himself, no, he must be tolerant. After all, Clancy could not choose his parents, nor insist they be married before his conception. Clancy's mother was a Mohawk…or Italian (one heard so many rumors in the Virginia Tidewater). Clancy's father had risen from pirate to privateer to governor's drinking companion in a matter of months. So why couldn't Clancy, just for once, conform? Only last year, Jefferson offered Clancy a good wage to survey lands west of Monticello. Clancy grinned, "Thanks, Tom, but if I venture too far from the sea, I evaporate." Jefferson could not converse with such an irrational creature. Clancy was fifty years old. When was he going to grow up?

"NO," Jefferson had to tell more than one visitor to Williamsburg, Virginia's capital, Clancy was NOT his "big brother." Yes, they both had red hair, but Clancy was a Redbeard, not a Randolph! Jefferson's hair was light red, like copper (or carrots, as his enemies liked to snicker), and neatly combed; Clancy's was wisps of fiery red sprinkled with white, as though with sea salt, and broke every comb it met. Jefferson wished Clancy would leave the country. Clancy's oldest brother, his legitimate half-brother Roderick, was the most successful slave trader in Virginia. Jefferson's father-in-law, also an importer of African slaves, had known and respected Roderick. Why didn't Roderick straighten Clancy out? Or put him on one of his ships and send him on a nice voyage to the far side of the world?

Jefferson knew he couldn't walk past Clancy unnoticed. Clancy could smell you six blocks away. He could see you from the opposite end of Duke of Gloucester Street without a spyglass. He could recognize the sound of your footsteps, and your horse's. If you shook his hand, he could tell by your calluses how long it was since you last played your violin, and with what bowing technique. Jefferson thanked the heavens that Clancy was too ne'er-do-well to use his supernatural senses for robbery or devilish trades, and was only interested in women, chocolate, women, wine, women, and women. Your wife and cellar weren't safe, but your purse was.

At least Clancy had the aesthetic sensibility to fill his glasses with clear rainwater, not swampy well water. Still, it was a disgrace, playing secular Händel in the middle of the day for women who should be tending their houses, children who should be at their studies, and a farmer and his bewitched horse who should be plowing something. And playing for money, with a tin box prominently displayed, into which Clancy had placed several coins: "Priming the kitty," he winked at Jefferson one day last year as he tuned his glasses. "Like The Reverend Harrison does with the alms box at Bruton Parish. Just so the audience gets the idea I'm not standing in the sun for my health." Clancy then purposely ripped one of his sleeves, and rubbed his cuffs with mud to make it look like he was too poor to afford a washerwoman (he was, but hired one anyway, for his wife Sarah hated doing laundry, and it was far more important she spend time educating their wee twin...even if all the stories she told them were warnings about never marrying the offspring of a pirate, or they too would suffer lives of misery and neglect).

Jefferson turned to his slave, or manservant, as was the polite term: "Jupiter! Let us to the wigmaker." Jefferson was materialistic and famished after the previous day's proclaimed Day of Fasting, Humiliation, and Prayer. The Virginia burgesses had called for the holy day to show solidarity with their loathed Massachusetts brethren to protest the Boston Port Act, a retaliatory punishment for Bostonians dumping the East India Company's tea into Boston Harbor the previous December. Virginians had to act. If Parliament could close the port of Boston, Norfolk might be next.

"Uh, Master Tom, the courts are closed," Jupiter said as delicately as he could, internally seething that Master Tom could be so absent-minded to forget that the Royal Governor,

Lord Dunmore, had dissolved the House of Burgesses in retaliation for the burgesses calling for that day of fasting and prayer – and with the courts closed, Jefferson's law practice about to end, his debts mounting, and the American colonies daring to oppose the world's most powerful empire, unless Master Tom's plan was to disguise himself with a blonde wig, it would be more prudent to visit the gunsmith.

"Very well," sighed Master Tom. "To the tailors." With his slim figure that showed off the latest fashions to their best advantage (and required half the fabric needed to shroud the typical corpulent Tidewater aristocrat), Jefferson was confident the tailor would happily wait for reimbursement. Scottish resident factors had extended easy credit to gentlemanly farmers like Jefferson, encouraging them to get into mind-boggling amounts of debt. Now, when Jefferson looked at Clancy, he saw not the bastard of a pirate, but something infinitely worse: a Glaswegian. Playing those ethereal musical glasses, Clancy resembled a Gaelic male siren, luring women to wreck themselves upon his loins.

Jupiter dug in his pockets for a coin and was about to put one in Clancy's tin box, when he saw Master Tom looking at him. Jupiter handed his hard-earned money to his master. Guests at Master Tom's ridiculously inconvenient and impractical house on a mountaintop gave the overworked Jupiter gratuities – not credit, aristocrats' currency, but actual coins.

Jefferson cleared his throat unnecessarily and made sure everyone saw him toss the coin into a glass, raising the water and, thus, lowering the pitch. Jefferson announced: "You may not be evaporating, sir, but your *C* is. A Portuguese Joe should prove the corrective."

"My *C* requires a small fleet of English gold coins!" Clancy smiled. *Or better yet, put the money IN THE TIN BOX.* Now, everyone would say how clever Mr. Jefferson was, and they'd all be tossing their smallest coins, or worse, rocks, into Clancy's tenor section, turning his musical performances into sporting events. He'd spend more replacing broken glasses than he'd earn and would be back looking for "real" work. *Besides, that glass was not out of tune, you tone-deaf know-it-all college clown*, Clancy thought. But Clancy couldn't make Tom look bad in front of others. If the burgesses ever reconvened, Jefferson would introduce a resolution to ban street musicians.

Jefferson suddenly remembered the rumor that Clancy had killed five men at the Battle of Culloden armed only with a broken whisky bottle. Jefferson hurried up the street to go shopping and get deeper into debt.

"Thank you, Mr. Jefferson!" Clancy called, putting a bandage on the situation. Without turning around, Jefferson lifted his hand in acknowledgement, and one war was averted. Two redheads butting heads would not have been a pretty sight.

An attractive woman in the crowd told Clancy, "You redheads are all devils."

"Aye," Clancy admitted, "but at least I'm not a lawyer."

Clancy was enraged that, in this day and age, Jefferson and his fellow burgesses were relying upon ecclesiastical tactics to get Americans out of this latest mess, calling for "a day of fasting, humiliation, and prayer, to implore divine interposition…" *Resolve to manufacture gunpowder, idiots! Closing Boston Port was ordained by man's laws, not God's. If the American colonists get into a holier-than-thou competition with the head of the Church of England (also known as George the Third), you had better establish a navy, fast…* But Clancy needed Jefferson's – or rather, Jupiter's – Portuguese Joes, so he held his tongue. Clancy supposed Händel had to remain silent in the face of stupid superstitious patrons so he, too, could pay his mortgage.

Clancy finished Minuet I, Suite I from *Water Music*. The crowd applauded, and the farmer's horse had seemed to enjoy it as well. Clancy had announced the work's name before he began. People got the joke; he got some coins.

Another acquaintance, Gowan, a black Baptist preacher, passed by. He was being led like a horse by a rope, pulled by two sheriffs, heading west towards the county jail. Still, that couldn't spoil Gowan's disposition. It was a glorious day, for

GOD was in the heavens, AMEN! "Morning, Clancy Redbeard!" Gowan called out.

"Morning, Gowan No Last Name! What are you in for this time?"

"Preaching without a license."

"Good on ye!" Clancy said.

Clancy knew he should play a popular tavern tune, like *Nottingham Ale*, or *Watkins Ale*, which would yield the most coins, but, above all things, he loved teaching. He split the difference and announced his next tune as *Mozart's Ale*, though Mozart called it *Molto Allegro* in his fourteenth symphony. Clancy had met the young Mozart in Paris in '63 and gotten him addicted to wine and cards. Clancy could take wine or leave it, though he preferred to take it, and cards were fine for making money, but to sit all night gambling, when there were women being neglected? Clancy hardly saw the thrill in that. Mozart apparently did. Mozart had a talented sister, Nannerl, who Father Leopold used as an accompanist for her brother. Clancy begged for Nannerl's hand, but Leopold refused to let Clancy marry his twelve-year-old daughter – and would refuse to let him marry her when she was twenty-two, thirty-two, and forty-two, "So give it up, Bastard of Redbeard!"

Clancy finished *Mozart's Ale/Molto Allegro*. The audience applauded politely but gave no coins. Applause did not impress nor feed his wife and twins. He'd have to cave into the mob's tastes by the end of day. But first, more Mozart!

"I will play you a motet, *God is our Refuge*, which I have rearranged as *A Ship is our Refuge*." Clancy winked, wet his fingers and played. *Ars gratia artis. Ars vincit pecuniam.* Old Widow Andrews, the town scold, walked by and let out a loud *huff!* at Clancy's impudence.

A soldier appeared. He was about forty – a major judging by his epaulettes, but Clancy did not recognize the regiment – with an old scar on his forehead: a clothes iron imprint, as though someone (a disgruntled woman, Clancy guessed) had tried to remove the wrinkles from his furrowed brow. He was toting a rifle. What was he doing in Williamsburg? And what was he hunting? The local Indians were subdued long ago....

The iron-burned major glared at Clancy's glasses. Did he overhear the quip about replacing God with a vessel? Turning a motet into a shanty was punishable by death in Massachusetts. Religious fanatics, you never knew where they were lurking. The major walked up to Clancy's table, and fished Jefferson's coin out of the *C*, correcting the pitch.

Clancy was euphoric: "Thank you, sir! It's rare to encounter a battle-scarred man who still possesses such an ear!"

Alas, the major did not put Jefferson's coin in Clancy's tin box; he pocketed it. He then picked up the *C* and drank the water.

As the major picked up the *F*, Clancy quipped, "Sir, that's water from the horse trough."

The major poured the water into the E-flat, turning it into a *D*. He knocked the middle *C* off the table, and it broke on the ground. The audience froze and said nothing. The major was lucky that Mrs. Vobe, the King's Arms Tavern proprietress, wasn't there. She had that large glass made specially for Clancy to lure customers into her establishment, and it cost a bloody fortune.

Clancy launched right into *A-Roving* in *D*, showing the major that nothing would make him stop playing.

"And the major obviously wishes me to play in a major key. I am only too happy to—"

With the butt of his rifle, the major bashed Clancy in the forehead. That made him stop playing.

The women in the audience gasped. The farmer and his horse ran away. Clancy wished Old Widow Andrews hadn't left. She was a nag, but she would have bashed the major right back: *she* ran Williamsburg, not him.

"Please," Clancy said, blood trickling down his nose. "I know you only enlisted because jobs are hard to come by—"

With the butt of his rifle, the major hit Clancy in the stomach.

Clancy doubled over. Blood dripped into his high *C*, turning the water crimson.

The entire audience ran away. Another soldier appeared, and they hauled Clancy up Duke of Gloucester Street, east, to jail.

II
BLACKBEARD'S HOST

*W*e once hosted Blackbeard! the Williamsburg jail guards loved to boast. When pressed for details, they admitted, *well, no, Blackbeard himself was never in the jail*, for he had met his end at sea...*but Blackbeard's skull visited Williamsburg!* where it was fashioned into a silver-plated drinking cup and put to good use at the Raleigh Tavern. Rather, it was Blackbeard's crew who spent a month in the jail before being taken a polite distance from town and hanged, every tree in Williamsburg having been cut down for firewood, housing, or in drunken fun. Merchants and tradesmen exploited any connection to the most famous pirate in the American colonies – far more famous than the Redbeard of Virginia, who had to share his nickname with Emperor

Frederick I and the Barbarossa Boys, those Barbary pirates. There were only so many hair colors: *Brunettebeard* didn't have much ring to it, and *Blondebeard* hardly inspired terror. Besides, Blackbeard warred with the governor of Virginia and died a glorious death in battle on his ship; Redbeard handed over sixty-three of his men to the governor, was pardoned of all past and future crimes, killed Shawnee and any Indian who crossed his path, reproduced himself unnecessarily, ruined countless women, became an old bore at parties, and died in his bed, having never spent a night in jail.

Now, all the Williamsburg jail could boast was Redbeard's Bastard. In most parts of the world, being the son of a pirate was scandalous enough; adding "bastard" was overkill, like saying *that man has smallpox…and pimples!* But Virginians will do anything to put others down a peg and keep them there. After all, Clancy's half-brother Roderick was now their social equal, and their superior in terms of wealth and influence. Who knew what bizarre turn of events could lift Clancy above them? So "Bastard of Redbeard" it was. Clancy kept his head down, as much as a musician could, and worked hard to not be a threat to anyone.

Virginians also enjoyed pointing out that Father Redbeard at least had the "decency" to marry Clancy's twenty-seven brothers' mothers (Redbeard attempted to double Blackbeard's record fourteen wives, and on his deathbed cursed himself for falling short by one). After retiring from piracy, Redbeard declared he would spread his seed to the four corners of the earth and have a different mother for each son. Alas, during one wedding party, he mistook one of his old wives for his new wife and impregnated her a second time. It was a mistake he would not repeat. From then on, each conquered woman who produced a healthy offspring – male, that is – was marked and numbered with a small brand on the back of her neck. Young Clancy asked his Shawnee mother what the *R20* signified. Clancy then suggested to Father that he give the mothers of his sons a nice gold ring for identification purposes instead of an agonizing burn. Father

Redbeard laughed and said it was the price women must pay for the pleasure of his company. Young Clancy quipped, "Well, as the pleasure seems to be all yours, you should be the one to pay!" After being slapped across the face and locked in the cellar, Clancy pried up the floorboards, found father's loot, took thirty gold coins, and gave them to Mother, and *R19* and *R21*, so the women could escape Father and find some nice husbands. When Redbeard learned what his little bastard did, Clancy was shipped off to a school in England, and Clancy never saw his mother and father again.

Clancy loved jail. A nice, friendly young guard, and you could sleep all you wanted! Clancy would have moved in permanently if not for the jail keeper, Peter Pelham. Pelham was also Bruton Parish's organist, and he always brought a prisoner from the jail to pump the organ – but never a Baptist: they could not refrain from shouting "AMEN!" every time The Reverend Harrison quoted scripture. Harrison wasn't willing to cut the bible out of his sermons, so Pelham was told to bring only Freemasons (like Clancy), atheists, or better yet, Hebrews, even though there were only two in the entire Tidewater, and both so law-abiding, unlikely to ever find themselves in Pelham's care.

At first, Pelham loved housing Clancy. An inmate with whom he could discuss Corelli, Haydn and Händel! But then Pelham asked Clancy, arrested yet again for disturbing the peace, to pump the organ. Having drunk three bottles of wine the previous evening, Pelham, in the middle of a service, ran outside to shit through his teeth, and Clancy stepped in, persuading Old Widow Andrews to pump for him. Parishioners exited the service marveling how Redbeard's Bastard played so much better than Pelham. Pelham had one of his guards "accidentally" step on three of Clancy's fingers, and so ended another potentially beautiful friendship.

Clancy considered working as a church organist in another town, but knew he'd never be able to stay awake during sermons and would miss cues. Clancy made most of his money playing on the streets. Occasionally, someone lent him a fiddle, or he sang, but the novelty of musical glasses proved the most lucrative. His wife, Sarah, wanted him to go back to surveying, his highest paying job, and the one that kept him away from home the longest. Clancy said all the land he was being hired to survey belonged to the Shawnee. Sarah threw a glass at him and wouldn't have sex with him for weeks. Second Floor Mary at the Raleigh Tavern got two visits from Clancy that month.

For a man of his years, drinking, and previous lechery, Clancy was superbly healthy. He still had all his teeth, fingers, toes, and other vital parts. He took the smallpox vaccination and got through it with one tiny pockmark on his shoulder. He once fell off the roof of Notre Dame and walked away with a sprained ankle. Clearly, the Almighty, or Allah, or the Fates intended him to do something.

When awake, Clancy planned. He longed to visit his daughter in Scotland. He wrote to her every week but hadn't a reply in four years. He suspected her mother, his second wife, was tearing up his letters, after taking out the money. He hoped his daughter knew he loved her, and he hoped his money wasn't being misspent by her mother's new drunken husband.

The young pockmarked jail guard loved Clancy: *a real live pirate!* "Tell me your adventures, Captain Redbeard!" Clancy didn't think any of his adventures (*bloody catastrophes*, he called them) had a moral. If there was one, he would have attempted to learn it himself and not make the same idiotic mistakes again and again and again. He preferred to teach the guard useful skills, like the art of tying knots. Clancy made up little stories to help his pupil remember the various steps: "The end of the rope is the snake. The snake goes into the loop, swims out to sea, but gets hungry and swims to France, going straight through the maze of rope that is Paris, slithers south to Auvergne...yes, perhaps too complicated a knot. Let's start with this simple one: here's the king's head," and Clancy made a loop. "Now, strangle the king." He wrapped the rope around the loop's neck. "Now, poke him in the eye." The guard laughed as Clancy jabbed the end of the rope through the loop.

"Thank you, Captain Redbeard!"

"I haven't been a captain in…" Clancy did the arithmetic: "…twenty years. Why didn't your father teach you this?"

"I don't know who my father is," the guard said, hanging his head.

"Well, then," said Clancy, putting his arm around the young guard's shoulder, "you must consider me as your father."

The guard thought it was too good to be true. He kept looking at Clancy's kind, battered face, waiting for the mocking laugh. It didn't come. Clancy meant it.

The horse-thief in the next cell quipped, "Knowing Clancy, he probably is your father."

"Could you be, Captain Redbeard?" the guard asked.

Clancy knew or was pretty sure he knew all his children. With women he didn't truly fancy, he couldn't come at all; with women he did, he usually went off at the first kiss. The rare times a woman gave him a second, or third, or fourth chance, and things proceeded well, he always took precautions. That one time, with his future wife Sarah, he was so drunk, his pigskin protection shot out of his hand, flew out the window and into a pasture, where it was promptly eaten by a goat – and Sarah could not wait a moment longer, and neither could Clancy. He didn't think he came close enough, but his twins said aye, he did. Whenever a woman told Clancy she wanted a child, he directed her to other men with steadier jobs and kinder bloodlines. But it was rude to reject the young guard's notion out of hand (plus Clancy drank so much, it was possible he might have forgotten one or seven children) so Clancy asked the guard, "You're seventeen?"

"As of last week," the guard said proudly.

Clancy did another calculation, charted the earth in his mind for his location at the time of the guard's conception, and sadly shook his head.

"I was in Italy. In jail."

"Piracy?"

"Lechery," Clancy boasted. "Until I can build an addition to the house, you'll have to share a room with my twins. They're going to love having a brother."

The guard threw his arms around Clancy. Clancy held his new son. "Just, please, don't call me Captain Redbeard. It reminds me of—"

They heard a door in the receiving room open. Clancy quickly stood and put his hands up so the guard could manacle him to the wall.

Was Thomas Jefferson the reason Clancy was in jail? Clancy never breathed a word about the affair, but those Gossips of the Tidewater... Before Thomas Jefferson and Patty were married, Clancy was there, reeling from the shock of hearing that his third wife had joined a nunnery. Patty played the spinet, and she and Clancy played together well. Clancy was thrilled when Patty informed him that if he were to propose to her, she would accept. But then Patty announced she would bring into the marriage her personal slaves and the one hundred-plus slaves she would inherit from her father – including her own six half-brothers and sisters. Patty treated her enslaved relatives better than Roderick treated Clancy (which wasn't saying much), but they would be her property; she could sell them to the West Indies if they didn't prepare her porridge just the way she liked. The situation made Clancy nauseated, and no matter how hard he tried, he could not get the disgustingness of it through Patty's thick, self-righteous skull. She saw nothing wrong with enslaving her own blood. Typical Virginian. Patty's father was a slave trader who frequently did business with Roderick. Clancy had hoped Patty was like himself, a thinking person striving to distance himself from the previous unenlightened generations. Alas... Clancy vowed to stop attempting to rescue women, or at least ask them, before taking any action, "Say, are you unhappy with your situation? Or do you get off on being waited upon by your enslaved sister/being beaten by your father/working as a prostitute...?" Clancy gave Patty one last French night to always regret him by. Before he cut and run in the dead of night, he put a note on her pillow: *Nice knowing you*. Then, realizing her maid might see it, burned it, and rewrote: *Nice meeting you*. See? Clancy could think, when he thought of it.

Nine hours after he left Patty's bedchamber, Clancy met his future wife, Sarah. Thomas Jefferson didn't consider that punishment enough? If the courts hadn't closed, Jefferson would be too busy to bother Clancy. There was nothing more villainous than a bored lawyer…except, perhaps, a bored woman.

Clancy asked the young guard, "Why am I in the public jail, and not the county jail with the Baptists? That's where I'm always put when they arrest me for disturbing the peace…"

Clancy realized he was being charged with some felony, not a misdemeanor. Would he receive mercy? The courts always laughed at the stories of his farcical mishaps fueled by his best intentions – or wine – and let him go; they didn't have many expectations for The Bastard of Redbeard. Clancy was harmless, and occasionally even useful to Williamsburg. He once repaired the courthouse steps without anyone asking. And he kept all the taverns in business.

The young guard ran out of Clancy's cell, slammed the door shut and locked it just as the door from the receiving room opened.

III
CLANCY IS HUNG…OR HANGED

Devlin, a nineteen-year-old boy in rags, sobbed as he stood before the judge.

"Dylan Devlin, you have been found guilty of piracy. It is the sentence of this court–"

"No! NO!" cried Devlin.

"–that you be hanged by the neck until you are dead, dead, dead. Have you anything to say?"

"I didn't know we was pirating! It was just like being in the Royal Navy."

In the Williamsburg capitol courtroom, the five spectators laughed. But they felt for the boy. He seemed sincere, and his story was probably true. After the *PATRICK DRISCOLL* was sunk with all hands lost, save for he, Devlin was rescued by a most interesting crew. The captain of the *KING'S PARDON* told him they were on a special mission for His Majesty George the Third. A ship that had no Marines and took no prisoners would save the Crown money, which His Gracious Majesty would then give to the poor needy mothers of Ireland…surely, young Devlin wanted to help the poor needy mothers of Ireland, like his own? *Of course, Captain!* Poor young gullible thing. So, the audience did not heckle Devlin as the bailiff pounded his tipstaff and two guards dragged the sobbing boy out.

The court had been closed since April, when the burgesses refused to renew the Fee Act, but this afternoon, ten regular court spectators looking for entertainment, debating whether to hurl taunts at the felons in the city jail or rotten fruit at the Baptists in the county jail, noticed the capitol court was hearing two special cases. But as they headed inside, a woman walked by selling strawberries.

Mr. Giddy, a lonely widower, stuck his head out the capitol door and told his fellow regulars, "They're trying the son of Redbeard!"

"He's the governor's pet," a woman snorted. "They'll give him a slap on the wrist. Besides, if he sees you gaping at him – or worse, his secretary sees you – they'll make your life a living hell. Have a strawberry."

"No, not Roderick Redbeard; Redbeard's bastard!"

The court regulars stuffed the strawberries into their cheeks and ran into the courtroom. A man walking by overheard, and soon a hundred people were fighting to get inside.

The judge looked at the bailiff and contemplated clearing the courtroom, but the mob was silent, and the judge rarely had such a large audience.

When Clancy, the most entertaining misdemeanoring man in Virginia, entered in manacles, the audience burst into applause. The bailiff pounded his tipstaff. Clancy smiled at his audience and blew kisses to them – difficult to do when one was manacled, but Clancy always managed acts of chivalry.

The bailiff proclaimed, "The defendant, Clancy, The Bastard of Redbeard, is charged with the crime of bigamy, that he did, on the first of June of this year seventeen seventy-four…."

Clancy breathed a sigh of relief. He thought he was being charged with horse theft, punishable by hanging. The previous week, when Patrick Henry stopped at the Edinburgh Castle Tavern for a drink, Clancy borrowed Henry's colt – only for five minutes, to race John Page to Christiana Campbell's Tavern and back, win two pounds, and return the colt. The poor thing needed some exercise. Mr. Henry should have paid Clancy for grooming and hot walking. Clancy reassured his worried admirers in the courtroom, "Bigamy? *Ha ha ha!* Why, in my youth – BIGAMY?!?"

Clancy's mind raced through his recent actions. "When?!" The audience laughed at Clancy's bad memory and the bailiff pounded his tipstaff.

"Call the witnesses," said the judge.

The bailiff called, "Sarah Redbeard and Mary Redbeard!"

Mary Redbeard? thought Clancy, mentally running through the short list of his still-living relatives. *Oh, that. But how did the court find out? Surely, not from Second Floor Mary. It was unlike her, and not just because she practiced an illegal trade and feared the authorities. Sarah? She wouldn't. Appearances were everything to her. A small gold snuffbox had bought the silence of the traveling Methodist clergyman who performed the hasty ceremony…* the sight of nut-brown Sarah and silver-and-pepper Mary, their beautiful hair framing their red-with-rage faces, stopped his thinking.

"That's him!" said Sarah. "That bastard is the one who—"

"Silence!" the judge ordered. "Wenches, how dare you come into this courtroom with your hair uncovered."

"Unlike other women in Williamsburg, I am not bald," Mary boasted, glaring at all the bonneted, mob-capped, and wigged women in the audience. The women booed her.

Sarah hissed at Mary, "And I am not diseased. Go back to the Raleigh Tavern and get back on your back, if your insides haven't shriveled up already."

The audience clapped and cheered. Clancy hated when Sarah, almost forty years old, acted like a jealous girl. He walked up to her and whispered, "Stop it. Show respect to an older woman."

Sarah was speechless. Clancy had never snapped at her like that, nor ever reprimanded her.

"Your Honor," Clancy said, "if I may be allowed to tell the tale, we could all go home in five minutes."

"You may hang yourself, Redbeard," the judge said, leaning back and closing his eyes for a nap.

Clancy turned and faced his audience.

"Ladies and gentlemen, Sarah and I were married for four years…four entire years…" The audience laughed at Clancy's regretful sigh. "Our union had gone sour – nay, turned to vinegar – just two days after we were wed, when Sarah and I realized we had not a thing in common, except a profound love of Madeira."

The self-righteous audience gave a collective *humph!*

Clancy continued, "Yesterday, I came home from work to find Sarah gone, and our crying twins alone in the house."

The audience booed and spat strawberries at Sarah. Clancy stepped in front of Sarah, glaring at the hecklers. They went silent, eager to hear the rest of his story. And they'd heard the rumors that The Bastard of Redbeard had killed six men at the Battle of Culloden armed only with a fork.

"I knew I had to do something," Clancy continued. "I took the twins and went to the Raleigh Tavern, upstairs to Miss Mary, with whom I had been very well acquainted before I met Sarah. And one night afterwards. All right, TWO!

"I knew Mary wanted children, which she herself was unable to bear, and for which she had been cruelly abandoned by her former husband. We went straight to the clergyman, were married, and went straight home with our two ready-made children. Imagine my surprise when I opened the door to find Sarah preparing supper, a bruise on her lovely white forehead. Not five minutes before I arrived home, the poor thing had gone down to the cellar to fetch some butter, bumped her head on a low beam, and was knocked out cold."

The audience howled. The bailiff pounded his tipstaff.

"Your Honor, I plead guilty to being such a poor husband that when my wife stepped out of the house for more than two minutes, I presumed she had abandoned me for a better man. As my incarceration would benefit no one, save Mr. Pelham – who, judging from the vanilla and saffron pudding he ate last night, is not hurting for money – I beg this court to release me so I may toil day and night to provide for Sarah and our twins, for Miss – er, Mrs. Mary Redbeard, for my second wife and daughter in Scotland, for the boy with the black skin and oriental eyes and his unscrupulous blonde blue-eyed mother who claims I'm his father, for my third wife who grew so disgusted with my concupiscence she ran off and became a nun, and in memory of my first, dearly departed wife. I beg you, nullify my marriage to Sarah, and uphold my marriage to Mary, so I may make her an 'honest woman,' though I object to women being labeled as not honest when men lie and make false promises to them."

The women in the audience applauded.

"What say you, Sarah Redbeard?" asked the judge.

"Hang him!" Sarah replied.

The audience groaned, "Nooooo..."

The judge turned to Mary. "Mary Redbeard, you do not want to be Clancy's wife, do you?"

"Oh, that's being impartial," Clancy said.

"Marry a man with one or two years left to him?" said Mary. "What is my gain? Nothing but the name of a once-famous pirate. Hang him!"

The audience groaned. The bailiff pounded his tipstaff. This was not going as Clancy had hoped. Clancy had been so eager to tell his story, he just now noticed how many things were amiss.

"Your Honor...where is my counsel? And how–"

Before Clancy could ask how the court was even in session, an out-of-breath messenger burst in, ran to the judge, and handed him a broadside:

REWARD for the Capture of Captain Rafe Naider and His Nefarious Band of Raiders – DEAD OR ALIVE, with a rendition of a brigantine.

The messenger gasped, "*JUSTICE* is coming. She's approaching Jamestown…"

The judge screamed, "Clear the court!"

The bailiff screamed, "Clear this court!"

The deputies pushed the baffled audience out. Guards grabbed Sarah and Mary and hauled them out.

"I'm not finished, Redbeard!" Sarah shouted, as the courtroom doors closed.

A guard gagged Clancy. The judge stood.

"Clancy, Bastard of Redbeard, you are sentenced to hang by the neck until you are dead, have you anything to say—"

The judge walked out. Clancy tried to scream. Two sheriffs grabbed Clancy. A deputy tried to grab Clancy's leg. With his foot, Clancy pushed the deputy across the courtroom. The deputy fell against the railing, breaking it. The bailiff struck Clancy in the head with his tipstaff. Clancy's knees buckled. Two deputies grabbed Clancy's legs, hoisted him up, and took him outside.

The usual place to hang the condemned was a mile outside town, just far enough away to have a parade and put on a bit of a show. But within the capitol's brick walls stood a hastily built gallows, with two ropes – one of them already occupied.

Clancy chewed through his gag. He couldn't die, not today. He hadn't saved enough money for Sarah and all his children! His roof needed patching! His daughter's doll was missing! "I demand a postponement until *JUSTICE* arrives!"

The guards dragged Clancy past the young pockmarked prison guard.

"Tell Sarah and Mary, I love them," Clancy said to his newly adopted son. "Tell them I'm sorry."

Devlin, the boy charged with piracy, dangled from the gallows, blue-faced.

Calvin, an enslaved black man standing on a ladder, repairing the brick wall, saw the guards taking Clancy to the gallows. Calvin waved frantically to the crowd standing near the capitol.

"They're hanging Clancy Redbeard! They're hanging Clancy!"

A guard shot Calvin in the neck, and Calvin fell off the ladder. All the men in the crowd fled. All the women ran to the capitol gate.

The young pockmarked guard pulled his pistol and pointed it at the guard holding Clancy's left arm. "Let him go! Let him go!"

Clancy said, "No, son, don't –!"

The guard holding Clancy's right arm pulled his pistol and shot the pockmarked guard in the face.

"NO! NO!" Clancy cried.

At the gallows, The Reverend Harrison, eyes tightly closed, raised his hands heavenward and wailed, "Heavenly father, pray forgive The Bastard of Redbeard, the spawn of the devil, the *AAAAAAHHRRGGHH*–" he concluded when Clancy kicked him off the platform.

Clancy begged the guards as they trussed him, "Please, let Sarah and my children come hang on me, so I may die quickly."

Old Widow Andrews, to whom Clancy had brought meals and jokes after her husband was killed in a carriage accident, ordered two women to bend over so she could step on their backs and climb to the top of the brick wall.

"Stop! Stop, you monsters!" she shouted.

A sheriff, thinking he could scare an old woman, pointed his pistol at her. Old Widow Andrews pointed her bony finger right back at him.

"Shame on you! Bad boy!"

The sheriff's hand shook, and he holstered his pistol.

A guard put a noose around Clancy's neck. Clancy looked up at the dark clouds. A lightning bolt streaked across the sky. Clancy prayed another bolt would hit him. It would be the quickest of deaths.

More women climbed up the brick wall, threw bricks, and began a chorus of "Murderers! Murderers!"

A guard went behind Clancy and kicked him off the platform.

Clancy dangled for three seconds –

– and then fell to the ground, landing on his feet.

"The rope broke!" shouted the women.

"It's a sign from God!"

"It's God's will!"

"It's a sign…!"

"God forgives The Bastard of Redbeard!"

"God, why…why?" moaned the Reverend Harrison.

A rope breaking was indeed a sign – that no one told the men who built the gallows that they were hanging two men that day, and they grabbed the first piece of rope they could find and had failed to test it. The judge was about to order the guards to find a new rope, but there was a mob of women armed with bricks, knitting needles, and strawberries glaring at him, and the judge's wife screamed at him any time he came home with the tiniest stain on his cravat.

As Clancy wriggled out of the rope pinning his arms and untied his gag, he heard a strange sound behind him. Clancy turned and looked up. It was the death rattle from young Devlin, hanging, blue-faced, neck broken, but still breathing.

Clancy turned to The Reverend Harrison and pleaded, "Put that boy out of his misery."

The Reverend kept silently praying to God to strike Clancy dead. Clancy turned to a guard.

"Please, help him!"

The guard spat on the ground and folded his arms.

Clancy grabbed the pistol out of the guard's holster and, with the butt end, smashed the guard in the face. Clancy turned, raised the pistol, and shot Dylan Devlin right between his eyes, ending the boy's suffering.

As the guards drew their pistols, the women knocked down the gate. The guards ran for their lives.

Clancy, all the while looking at the young dead pockmarked guard, was surrounded by the women, and pushed out into the street.

"The Lord be praised!"

"It's a sign from God!"

"God blesses the bastard!"

The judge, hiding behind a tree with The Reverend, said, "Next time, we burn him at the stake."

IV
NAIDER'S RAIDERS

Clancy smelled like the jail, and had a noose around his neck and no money. The women of Williamsburg got a good whiff of Clancy and went home, satisfied that he would live to entertain them another day.

Clancy stood outside the Raleigh Tavern, throwing pebbles at a second-floor window. He picked up a rock, threw it, and knocked over the bust of Sir Walter Raleigh sitting on the ledge above the front doors.

"Mary! Mary! Mary Redbeard!"

Clancy picked up a bigger rock and threw it, breaking a window. As Clancy looked at Shield's Tavern across the street, wondering if Mary had taken up employment there, the Raleigh tavern keeper leaned out a second-floor window and dropped a bucketful of water on Clancy. Few things made Clancy scream, but unexpected dousings and dunkings did. He didn't know why. Some bad forgotten memory, perhaps…at least now he smelled better.

Clancy ran to the jail to make sure Mary was not there. Pelham told him the judge had a change of mind: he decided a prostitute lacked the brains to act reasonably, as did The Bastard of Redbeard, and the entire matter had been dropped. Clancy breathed a sigh of relief. Pelham asked Clancy if he wanted a job; the young pockmarked guard's position was suddenly available. Clancy walked away before Pelham could see him cry.

"Why did God let those poor boys die, and let me live?" Clancy asked the air. "Where is the justice?"

The *JUSTICE* came up the York River and docked at the tobacco port. His Raiders wanted Captain Naider to speak at Jamestown because of its historical significance as the first permanent English settlement, but Naider said that swamp's air was unhealthy, and Yorktown had more wealth and, hence, corruption.

Clancy first saw Naider speak in Philadelphia when they were both young men. Clancy voraciously read Naider's pamphlets and articles in the gazettes – always signed RAFE NAIDER, his real name, in a time when no "gentleman" signed his, except to advertise for runaway horses and slaves. Rafe Naider, Benjamin Franklin, and Captain Death formed Clancy's Trinity. Clancy admired Jesus, too, but preferred to focus his attention on men he might have a chance of aiding. Knowing how Naider always followed the money, Clancy ignored what the messenger told the judge, and got a ride to Yorktown from the farmer and the horse that liked his musical glasses.

On at least twenty occasions, Clancy had begged Naider to let him join the crew of the *JUSTICE*, though most men would find jail preferable: one meal a day, long, long hours, little or no pay, leaky ship, and worst of all, an ever-growing detestation by the public. Naider told Clancy, "I need men who have the ability not to be loved!" That was not Clancy. If Clancy's mother had given him one pat on the head every day, he would have never gotten into so much mischief purely to get attention. If Sarah had kissed Clancy's cheek once a week, he would have eschewed alcohol, taken that surveying job Thomas Jefferson offered him, and never visited Mary again.

Naider was born in the hills of Connecticut near the Berkshires. Father Naider, a hard-working businessman in Lebanon, fled the piratical Ottoman Empire and sailed to America, setting up a successful bakery-tavern west of Hartford. Father Naider loved Robert the Bruce and the Great Highland Bagpipe, and was such a Scotsophile, he named his bakery-tavern The Highland Arms. Son Rafe inherited his father's soft spot for the Scots, hence his never-ending patience with Clancy. Naider was sure Clancy would come around and really do something, one day.

Why couldn't Naider have quit in his prime, gotten fat, and married an heiress? He would be the most beloved man on earth – even more than Benjamin Franklin! Naider's contemporaries had quit the battlefield long ago, nagged by wives and children for luxuries like regular meals and remembering their names. A few old Raiders now owned plantations and slaves and were filthy stinking rich. They occasionally sent Naider a few coins to alleviate their guilt. He made them look bad, selfish. They were starting to turn on him. They begged him to retire: "Why risk damaging our legacy?" they whined. Naider only cared about justice and was willing to endure ridicule and sacrifice his reputation. But now his enemies had him on the run, with trumped-up charges and endless bogus lawsuits.

It was Naider who, beginning with the 1764 Sugar Act, led the campaign to stop purchasing British goods: "Vote With Your Purse!" It had worked: non-importation and non-consumption agreements were easy to organize, created coherence within a community, and kept corrupt businessmen restrained. For a few years, ordinary citizens realized it was fun to fight your oppressors. You didn't need a pedigree, or even much money. Nevertheless, every few months, Parliament trotted out a new act, and the colonists' money flowed back into their coffers. Unscrupulous merchants painted Naider as an enemy not of parliamentary greed and corruption, but of every business: the frugal, plain-dressed lawyer simply didn't want anyone to own nice things or have any fun. Why, not buying things was downright disloyal, unpatriotic – *treasonous!*

With the never-ending libels in the press, Naider's star was tarnished. He wouldn't sink to responding to such obvious defamation. Alas, gullible citizens mistook the claptrap for actual news and parroted everything they read in the gazettes, especially the label, "Naider Traitor." Naider sighed, "I don't particularly care for the name, but at least 'Naider Raider' rhymes," and he went back to his lawsuits.

Justice was Naider's favorite word. Charmed by a traveling sculptor's tiny donation, Naider commissioned him to carve a figurehead of the Roman goddess Justice. The sculptor carved a blindfolded woman holding a set of scales, but no sword: "That will be extra," the slimy sculptor shrugged. "Very time-consuming to carve." Areebah, Naider's ever-exasperated daughter, said the scales weren't hydrodynamic, and the blindfolded woman would be interpreted as a signal that the Raiders didn't know where the hell they were going. Kelvin, Naider's chief legal advisor, wanted a better figurehead: "A bare-breasted woman – now *that* would attract crowds. And if she had really big, firm breasts, other ships would be too busy gawking to fire at us." Naider waved them both off, and told the sculptor to forget the sword: what message did it send when a safety advocate began brandishing weapons?

Clancy took a step back as *JUSTICE* approached. She bumped into the pier, crushing five boards.

Kelvin and Areebah swung on ropes off the ship and landed on the pier, wearing the Raiders' signature black frock coats and breeches, black stockings, and black cocked hats. Areebah was thirty-five, Arab to the hilt, tall and athletic, a haversack hanging from her shoulder. She marched up the pier. Most men would have bowed and displayed their calves, but with all the falsies men wore, women had grown cynical. And Clancy was not most men. Instead, Clancy smiled, flashing his rare possession: white teeth. Areebah did not stop to admire them.

When he landed on the pier, fifty-year-old Kelvin winced and rubbed his knee. He had wild white hair as though lightning hit him (it had, twice), was half Arab, half Scottish. Somehow, neither Raider had crossed paths with Clancy, though they'd both spent countless evenings laughing at Rafe's stories about the pirate's son who got himself into one hilarious scrape after another.

Piracy was a charge slapped on anyone the Crown disliked, and Naider could have made a career solely from defending innocent men accused of it. Tomorrow was their big chance to make legal history. Kelvin addressed Clancy as he limped up the pier: "Sir! An innocent man is about to be hanged. Which way to Williamsburg?"

Clancy pointed to his noose.

Kelvin growled, and bellowed, "Areebah! God has intervened."

Areebah turned, saw the man in his noose waving to her, and hurled her haversack into the river. She cooled down by fishing it out with a tree branch. Kelvin kicked the pier. "So much for setting a precedent!"

"I apologize for living," said Clancy.

Areebah said, "God – or your friends – breaking your noose is not a legitimate escape. What kind of legal swampland is this?"

"Virginia," said Clancy. "By the way, I was not innocent. I did commit bigamy."

"BIGAMY?" said Kelvin and Areebah in unison. Kelvin huffed, "They said you were charged with piracy!"

Areebah said, "Bigamy may be a felony in Virginia, but they always let men off the hook. Exactly how many women did you make miserable – I mean, marry?"

"Why did they hang you, Mr. Devlin?" asked Kelvin.

"Because I'm Clancy."

"Clancy? The Bastard of Redbeard?"

Now Clancy bowed. Areebah and Kelvin also bent over, with laughter. Kelvin got an extra surprise when he shook Clancy's hand: a brother Freemason. "Rafe's told us stories!"

"I'm delighted to hear I've been a source of amusement on long voyages."

"We should use you as our figurehead. I'm Kelvin, and that's–" Kelvin looked at Areebah. "Well, I suggest you keep your distance."

Areebah said, "Pirates are supposed to be tried by a court of Vice-Admiralty, not the General Court. Has Virginia gone mad?"

"What did you expect?" Kelvin asked. "Here, they marry their cousins and enslave their own progeny."

Sober young men in dark coats lowered the anchor. Kelvin bellowed, "Rafe! RAFE! We're at Yorktown!"

Clancy said, "Justice...always a day late and a shilling short. Well, if Mr. Devlin's trial was anything like mine –"

"There was a trial?" Kelvin mused. "That's good. That's very good news."

"Good?" Clancy asked.

"The British have been hanging pirates on the spot."

Clancy was incredulous. "The boy is still dead!"

Kelvin, not without feeling but, like a doctor who could not afford to get swallowed up in mourning his patients, pressed ahead. He called up to a young Raider, "We need a crowd!"

The Raider blew *Naider's Call* on a battered horn to announce their arrival, and while Kelvin and Areebah rounded up an audience, Clancy climbed aboard.

The gun ports were tarred shut, and the cannon sold long ago to hire more lawyers. *JUSTICE* was the most fired-upon ship on the seven seas, but no one could sink her. Once, off the coast of Mexico, she was cannonballed and was about to sound when a pod of killer whales saw her helplessness and, like a mother pushing her calf to the surface, kept *JUSTICE* afloat long enough so the Raiders could pump water from her hull, make repairs, and sail to the Galápagos Islands and, finding no one there to sue, sail to Japan to fight for pensions and free ear-trumpets for retired female pearl divers. The *Virginia Gazette* reported the story, so it had to be true.

Clancy wondered if, when the inevitable day came that *JUSTICE* finally foundered, the Raiders would be swallowed by a great fish and spat out on the dock in Philadelphia. He could envision them, leaping to their feet and striding to City Tavern without stopping to shake the fish phlegm off their black suits, and slapping a lawsuit on Benjamin Franklin and his dangerous electric turkey cooker, which lacked a safety bar to protect small children – or indeed, Dr. Franklin – from electrocuting himself.

Rafe Naider sat hunched over his desk in the middle of the deck, a stack of papers under a cannonball paperweight (a gift from a Spanish merchant ship). The occasional paper wafted off the desk and into the sea. The young crew in black paid no attention to Clancy. Naider said in his friendly voice, "Hallo, son of Redbeard."

Clancy sat next to Naider. "Captain Naider, thank you for never including the word *bastard* in your salutations."

Naider kept writing. "I prefer *Clancy of Culloden*."

"I should thank my father, I suppose. He didn't have to acknowledge me, let alone give me his name. It has opened many doors for me, though most were later slammed in my face when I failed to follow in his footsteps. One would think one's hosts would be overjoyed when the son of a pirate refrained from raping their wives, setting their house on fire, and pilfering the silverware."

"You disappointed them! People invite you over to liven things up!" Naider saw the noose round Clancy's neck. "The latest fashion?"

"Aye, your crew will all be wearing them soon."

Naider kept writing. "I have to finish this brief."

Clancy leaned over and looked at Naider's papers. "You're suing John Dickinson, again?"

"He's endangering his neighbors by refusing to install a lightning rod on his house, just because Benjamin Franklin invented it."

"Benjamin Franklin…" Clancy said, looking up at the sun's rays bouncing off the lightning rod on *JUSTICE's* mainmast. "*Would not these pointed rods draw the electrical fire silently out of a cloud before it came nigh enough to strike, and thereby secure us from that most sudden and terrible mischief! Behold, He spreads His lightning about Him, and He covers the depths of the sea.*"

"Clancy, you must become a lawyer!"

Not this again! "That was Dr. Franklin and Job, chapter thirty-six, verse thirty – not me!"

"Be a lawyer!"

"Do you know how old I am? Endure a two-year apprenticeship? In two hours, I could crack John Dickinson upside the head and install the lightning rod myself! Your faith in me is greatly appreciated, if terribly misplaced. Who would hire me? Rich merchants? Criminals? But I repeat myself."

Naider said, "With your wealth, you could represent the poor."

"Wealth?"

"Your father left you his plantation, fifty-two slaves, and twenty thousand pounds."

Before Clancy could reply, Areebah climbed aboard. "Dad, the coast is clear. Lieutenant Owens told the authorities we were landing at Jamestown."

"So, this is the beautiful daughter you keep hidden away," smiled Clancy. For years, he'd heard rumors that she was so ugly, Naider kept her below deck filing papers. Clancy realized Naider probably started those rumors to keep annoying suitors, like himself, at bay.

"Areebah, this is Clancy."

Clancy stood and touched the imaginary brim of his lost hat. Areebah did not lower her eyes nor curtsey.

"*Areebah!*" said Clancy. "Arabic for *witty and smart.*"

"Yes," said Naider, "and she has a gun."

Areebah patted her pocket and grinned. Clancy sat back down.

It was late afternoon, when everyone in town was hungry and wanted to go home. The sheriffs, if they were at Jamestown, had over twenty miles to travel in the dimming light. Plenty of time for a speech. Naider went to his lectern – the ship's bow – and arranged his papers. Clancy stood with the audience.

They either remembered his good deeds, or had heard he had once done good deeds, or they just wanted to see someone new. Mothers, farmers, shopkeepers, and a barber and his half-shaved client listened to Rafe Naider speak from the bow of *JUSTICE*: "…Virginia must end her dependence upon tobacco, a crop with severe consequences for the health of the soil, let alone the health of the consumer, let alone the health of the enslaved workers who toil to grow that tobacco.

"By discouraging domestic manufacturing, Parliament has turned us into a consumer society. Colonists are subjected to the whims of British merchants, forced to buy substandard goods that cause personal injuries. Behemoth manufacturers stifle American industry and ingenuity. Here in Yorktown, Rogers' Pottery once manufactured bird bottles to encourage Purple Martins to nest in Williamsburg and consume mosquitoes, and thus save the Virginia capital from going the way of the former capital, that swampland known as Jamestown – but Rogers was forced to downplay the size of his business to avoid the wrath of monopolizing merchants in England. Parliament thinks Americans backward, and that we will never unite against their corruption–"

A tobacconist called out, "Naider, this is treason!"

Clancy thumped the tobacconist's head. "Is he advocating killing George the Third? NO! Listen!"

Naider continued, "Small farmers are the heart of America, but they cannot compete against colossal plantations that employ enslaved labor…"

A young seamstress tugged Clancy's sleeve. "What are they?" she asked, pointing to Naider and his Raiders. "Pirates?"

"Worse. Lawyers."

Naider continued, "The Scottish economist Adam Smith said, quote, *People of the same trade seldom meet together even for merriment and diversion, but the conversation ends in a conspiracy against the public or some contrivance to raise prices*, end quote. Businessmen love to rig markets. Adam Smith has a book coming out soon that you all must read. Areebah, what's the name of his book?"

"*Samuel Johnson is a Big Fat Idiot.*"

Naider continued, "General Thomas Gage, the new governor of the Province of Massachusetts Bay, said in an intercepted letter to his superior, Barrington, quote, *Democracy is too prevalent in America, and claims the greatest attention to prevent its increase*, end quote. It is seventeen seventy-four; high time to change our society from an aristocracy to a meritocracy…"

It was almost sunset and Naider had lost most of his audience, except the tobacconist who rarely got a chance to heckle anyone, and two women whose husbands always bawled them out when they got home, so why not make them wait a little longer? Naider was momentarily thrown by chopping sounds coming from below him. Once, in Rhode Island, in the middle of his speech, a woman took an axe and chopped the legs off his platform. He'd leapt off just in time.

As Naider spoke, Clancy chiseled away Justice's blindfold, giving her eyes, and knocked Justice's unhydrodynamic scales into the river. Areebah almost grinned.

Naider said, "Charity is important, but justice is prevention. A society that has more justice needs less charity. When are we going to wake up and–"

The tobacconist shouted at Naider, "You're defying God by putting that Franklin Rod on your ship – God wants that ship destroyed!"

Clancy shouted at the tobacconist, "You're defying God by wearing spectacles – God wants you to walk off a cliff!"

Naider carried on. "The credit crisis of seventy-two–"

A man behind the tobacconist shouted, "Disperse at once!"

Kelvin and Areebah looked at the new heckler, and saw it was a Royal Navy officer. The tobacconist and the two women ran away. Clancy grabbed the head rail and swung himself out of view.

Lieutenant Owens marched down the pier, twenty broadsides under his arm, and climbed aboard

Clancy peeked over the railing, watching Raiders run below deck. Owens dumped the *REWARD for the Capture of Captain Rafe Naider and His Nefarious Band of RAIDERS – DEAD OR ALIVE* broadsides onto Naider's desk.

Owens said, "The only reason I'm not arresting you is because I remember what you did for my father."

"How many times did his carriage flip over going down that hill? Six?"

"Eight."

"See? Seatbelts should be mandatory!"

"Go to Florida."

"Florida?!"

"Or some uninhabited island. Create a new country with your own laws."

"We do not need new laws," said Naider. "We need to enforce the existing laws."

"Join William Death, if he still lives."

Clancy's spirits lifted at the mention of his third hero's name. *Yes! They should join Captain Death!*

"William is welcomed to join us," said Naider, "if he's willing to work within the law."

"Your revolution is dead, Naider."

Clancy popped his head up from the ship's railing, singing, *"Naider's Raiders are going to sue you..."*

Owens pulled his pistol and fired at Clancy. Clancy ducked just in time.

"If I ever see that felon on this ship again, I'll blow

JUSTICE out of the water. Make sail!"

Lieutenant Owens climbed off the ship. Clancy hopped over the railing onto the deck. Raiders prepared to sail.

Naider sighed. "Come, Clancy. We'll take you to Philadelphia – if you comb your hair, so you'll pass for one of the crew."

"Only if you make me a Raider," Clancy said. "I can do carpentry, navigation, fashion a sword for Justice – anything you need."

"I need more lawyers! And money! If you trip over any rich people in your travels, imitate your father and relieve them of their cash," Naider took his paperwork and went below deck.

As Naider was almost always right, Clancy pondered if he should pilfer silverware and jewelry, give the proceeds to Naider, and Naider would do something. Clancy and Naider agreed on all matters, but parted ways when it came to strategy. "There's a reason people admire pirates," Clancy called down to Naider. Clancy thought he was not worth endangering *JUSTICE and* disembarked. Besides, it would take three days to detangle his hair.

As Clancy climbed off the ship, Areebah came down the pier. She looked great in breeches. *I'd like to have her back against mine in a gunfight,* Clancy thought. He blocked her path and smiled.

"Why is a beautiful woman hanging around a bunch of lawyers?"

"Why is a useless bastard hanging around a crusader?"

The blood left Clancy's loins. He stepped aside, and watched Areebah climb aboard. Clancy was glad her buttocks were as flat as pancakes. He thought he could probably forget ever meeting her.

JUSTICE pulled away from the dock. Areebah saw Kelvin standing on the pier, hands on his hips, looking inland.

"Kelvin!" Areebah yelled, waving him to come aboard.

"I'm going to find out what's going on here. I'll catch up with you in Philadelphia," Kelvin said, having no idea how he'd get to Philadelphia, but one more night spent on *JUSTICE,* and he would have mutinied himself.

"We're going to Boston – BOSTON!" shouted Areebah.

"There's nobody here!" Kelvin shouted back, pointing to the deserted dock. It was the Raiders' custom to broadcast the wrong destination to fool their enemies. It usually worked. Of course, they also fooled their admirers, who would have gladly shown up and donated had they known where the hell *JUSTICE* was.

JUSTICE sailed into the moonrise. Kelvin was the only Freemason on Naider's ship and was glad to spend time with a brother. Kelvin tuned to Clancy and drew his sword.

"To arms!"

Clancy and Kelvin "borrowed" two horses and rode to the King's Arms.

V

THE KING'S ARMS

Clancy attempted to play *Chester*, but Kelvin kept emptying the wine glasses before Clancy could get them in tune. While Clancy apprised Kelvin of events in Williamsburg, the other patrons of the King's Arms Tavern stared at Kelvin in terror. Never mind the Indians, the French, Spanish pirates, and smallpox; there was nothing more deadly than a Naider Raider. The *Virginia Gazette* said so, so it had to be true. But when Mrs. Vobe, the proprietress and Clancy's musical glass patroness and a woman smart enough not to believe everything she read in the *Virginia Gazette,* saw that

Clancy was friendly with a Naider Raider, she tore up Clancy's bill for all the broken glasses, and Clancy got a hot bath, a new suit from a guest who had shot himself the previous week, supper, and all the drinks he wanted.

Mr. Dandridge, an affable eighty-year-old gentleman, opened the front door – or rather, his slave opened it – and saw Kelvin.

"That's one of Naider's Raiders," Dandridge gasped.

Kelvin bellowed, "Damn Rafe Naider and the leaky boat he rode in on!"

Dandridge smiled with relief, entered, and everyone in the tavern relaxed, resumed eating, and talked about how much they despised Naider and who did that arrogant Arab think he was trying to make things safer and how dare he interfere with God's grand scheme, if people were so stupid as to let their carriages hit a stone in the road, they deserved to die! It was Providence's way of getting rid of the weak, who might reproduce themselves…!

"Are you leaving Naider?" Clancy asked Kelvin.

Kelvin shook his head. "Although I am praying that *JUSTICE* sinks. Naider's Raiders' days of glory are over. We should have sailed off into the sunset while we were still popular in the sixties. It's difficult for rebels not to wear out their welcome. Imagine if Robin Hood kept taking from the rich and giving to the poor after Richard the Lionheart was back on the throne."

Clancy affected a whiny upper-crust English accent: "*All right, Robin, enough already – put that royal deer down!*"

Kelvin whispered, "Speaking of kings, Louis the Fifteenth is dead."

Few things made Clancy put down a drink. That did. "Mon dieu! Louis-Auguste is…?"

"Mmm hmmm…"

"A nineteen-year-old boy on the throne of France–"

"Highly impressionable…"

"Louis-Auguste loves ships. The French Navy–"

"And who will be his foreign minister?"

"Vergennes," grinned Clancy.

"The enemy of my enemy is my new best friend—"

Clancy stomped his feet like an excited five-year-old. "They'll declare war on England."

Clancy and Kelvin raised their glasses and roared, "GOD SAVE THE KING!"

"GOD SAVE THE KING!" cried out the other patrons of the King's Arms.

Clancy asked Kelvin, "If you think Naider's day is over, why are you still with him?"

Kelvin sighed. "My wife has *ideals*. The little ball and chain owns her own business, she doesn't like fancy clothes, she doesn't like jewelry—"

"Does she have a sister?" Clancy asked.

"—she insists I do something to end slavery…God, why did I marry a virtuous woman? All I wanted to do was stick it to the Crown and make a lot of money. So, I became a lawyer. I should have been a pirate. It would have been more fun, and more honest. Worst mistake I ever made was when William Death wrote to me and asked me to join his crew and I, in an over-educated Harvard-induced haze, said no!"

"William Death...*Captain Death*," Clancy smiled.

"You've sailed with him?"

Clancy shook his head. "My father knew him. Captain Death must be very, very old..." Clancy leaned forward and whispered, "Is it true Benjamin Franklin is William Death?"

Kelvin laughed. "If you ask him, Ben will just take a long, deep breath and smile." Kelvin slammed the table with the palm of his hand. "Speaking of women…."

"Were we?" Clancy thought he'd better stop drinking for the night, if he couldn't follow Kelvin's line of thought. Clancy looked around the tavern to see if there was a woman with whom he could keep company that night. "All the women here are with other men."

"That wouldn't have stopped your father," said Kelvin.

Two sheriffs opened the tavern door, saw Clancy, and were about to charge in, when they saw Kelvin. Kelvin pushed his chair back so they could get a good look at his sword, two pistols, and dagger. The sheriffs backed out, their spurs jingling as they ran to their horses.

"I suggest we depart," said Kelvin.

Gowan No Last Name, the oft-arrested Baptist preacher, came to their table. He was owned by Mrs. Vobe and working his official position as tavern server. Tavern slaves were the most reliable gazettes:

"Gowan," Clancy whispered. "Any news of Captain Death?"

"Word is he was killed in South Carolina, trying to free Edward Rutledge's slaves."

Gowan took Kelvin's hand and put coins in it.

"For what you did in Savannah. God bless you and Rafe Naider."

"Thank you, sir."

Clancy grinned, "What about me, Gowan?"

Gowan took their empty glasses and went back to the kitchen. Gowan liked Clancy, but the Raiders did something. In Savannah, they saved four falsely accused black men from hanging. True, the men were hanged the next day by an angry mob, but the Raiders had set a precedent. And how many white men ever stood up for blacks? It was a start.

Kelvin admired the coins. "So, I am not walking to Philadelphia! I mean Boston. Boston…" Kelvin handed a coin to Clancy. "And you, Clancy Redbeard, are off to enjoy the company of the Raleigh Tavern's second floor."

Clancy sighed, "No. I must do something."

VI
LAUGHINGSTOCK OF THE SEVEN SEAS

The next morning Clancy threw open the door, holding a bouquet, a doll, and a toy cannon.

"Daddy's here!"

Clancy was proud of his house. It had three rooms – two more than most houses in Williamsburg – wood floors (most had dirt), books, and a fine cellar. Clancy had studied drainage systems in Amsterdam, and on this swampy Virginia peninsula, it was the only cellar that never flooded. If only he had figured out how to move that low beam that knocked Sarah out cold, the whole bigamy thing could have been avoided.

But Clancy hated staying in one place for more than a few months, and so far from water – almost four miles from the James River, and over fifty from the sea. The house was beginning to feel like a jail in which he was only allowed to sleep three or four hours on the rare peaceful night. His father's piratical blood and his Shawnee mother's culture of moving with the seasons made Clancy long for continuous travel. But the Shawnee wanted nothing to do with The Bastard of Redbeard, whose father had tried to annihilate them, and that little incident on the Thames, when he ran his ship into London Bridge, made Clancy the laughingstock of the seven seas – not to mention the Potomac, Nile, Yangtze, Amazon, Volga, Congo, and Mississippi.

Clancy's four-year-old twin daughter and son screamed, leapt from the table, and ran to Daddy. Clancy knelt and handed his daughter the doll, and his son the toy cannon. Clancy bellowed the piratical laugh he knew they loved, "*HA HA HA!* These be my children!" and then turned serious. "These *are* my children. Always use correct grammar, my dears; people will think you a lady and gentleman, and you'll get away with murder, just like your grandfather."

The twins clambered to get the biggest hug. Oh, they were sweet things, always so forgiving. If only grown women could be like them. "My angels! My sweet darlings...don't worry, my heart is so big, there is room for both of you."

"And your head is so empty, you could fit a whole orphanage in there," snapped his wife Sarah, laboring over the Franklin stove. Clancy almost screamed when he saw her wearing his Masonic apron, covered in grease stains, but Clancy wanted sex, so he bit his tongue.

Clancy rocked his children. "I am proud that I brought you into this world, even if your mother did most of the work, and my end took but ten seconds."

"Five," said Sarah.

"You were counting?" Clancy pulled his twins close and whispered to them, "I was in a hurry to have you, my loves."

"Out!" said Sarah. "OUT!"

The twins took their presents and ran out the front door.

"Not you – *him!*" Sarah shouted, pointing her spoon at their no-good father, but they had fled.

Clancy wondered if all the women who claimed their

children were his were telling the truth, especially that blue-eyed blonde woman in Barcelona who produced the black boy with oriental eyes. *But who knew with whom or what my ancestors lay*, thought Clancy, and he dutifully if not happily handed over the contents of his purse. With the twins, there was no doubt. They looked like tiny versions of him, which made Sarah grit her teeth every time she laid eyes on them. Clancy had no choice; he had to straighten up, lest she take her rage out on them.

Clancy stood, massaged his creaky knees, and grabbed Sarah. "Did I really last an entire five seconds? You try going to sea for three years with a bunch of stinking men and see how long you last when you disembark," and he kissed her passionately. She dropped her spoon on the floor. Clancy ripped off her – his – apron and tossed it onto the Franklin stove, where it promptly caught fire.

Clancy swooped Sarah up and was about to make for the bedroom when he saw, sitting at his place at the table, spoon frozen in mid-slurp, the iron-burned major who attacked his musical glasses.

Clancy knew he should do something: hurl an insult, glove across the face, fire poker through the eye…but sweeping Sarah off her feet had wretched his back. *Serves me right*, thought Clancy. *Look how quickly I replaced Sarah when I thought she had left me*. What Clancy really wanted to do was break down and cry, but Sarah was the sort of woman who, upon seeing any weakness in her husband, would instantly leave him for another man…but she had apparently already done that. Clancy's muscles went limp, and he unintentionally dropped Sarah on the wood floor. Sarah picked herself up, marched into the bedroom and slammed the door.

Clancy turned to the iron-burned major. "One moment, sir."

Clancy picked up his bouquet, took a deep breath, went into the bedroom, and slammed the door. The major, exhausted from slaughtering Indians in Ohio, beating up street musicians, being scolded by Sarah, and truly enjoying his soup, resumed eating.

I t had not been Clancy's intention to marry a hog farmer's shrewish daughter. He had simply grown tired of stupid young girls who agreed with everything he said. He wanted a challenge. He had heard that Sarah was a feisty woman who had rejected every other man (*because she was waiting for an intelligent, worldly and unique man, like me!* Clancy fancied). Clancy thought sex with her would be wonderful, vigorous exercise after standing in one place all day playing his musical glasses. Alas, a night of ecstasy, or even five seconds of ecstasy, was never without long-term consequences. Apart from having no sense of humor, Sarah disagreed with everything he said simply for the sake of disagreeing, and there was no rhyme nor reason to her arguments; she would constantly contradict herself.

It was hard to hate Clancy – he always brought home good food, and took care of the house and the twins – but Sarah was determined to do it, and inflict as much pain on him as he had on her: what kind of man impregnates a women in their first "coupling"– he wasn't even a tenth of the way in – with TWINS? And then refuses to take a steady job with predictable income? Clancy suggested he take the twins off her hands and find another woman who would love them, like Mary; why punish the dear little things for one night of drunken carelessness? Was Sarah more interested in hurting Mary than helping her children? Evidently, yes. *Fine – if not Mary, then give them to some other childless woman.* What, give MY children away? *Yes! You obviously despise the little Redbeards…* The fight spiraled down and around, never ending.

Clancy joined the Freemasons to become a better man, to stay virtuous, and to work on the ever-elusive temperance and prudence (though there was little evidence of temperance in the lodge), but all the things his Masonic brothers told him to do to be a better husband only made things worse. When Clancy announced he was going to be a better husband by skipping that week's lodge meeting so he could stay home and help with the cleaning, it provoked months of ridicule from his "brothers" (with brothers like them, who needed Roderick?), and it hadn't pleased Sarah (so what if he got the job done – he didn't clean things *the right way!*).

Clancy had once taken a steady job, at Sarah's father's hog farm. After three days of enduring his father-in-law and coming home in such a rage that his angry visage made the twins burst into tears, Clancy quit. He went back to playing his glasses, the twins' smiles returned, and Sarah's left for good. Clancy could not figure out how to fix this terrible domestic situation and feared the only way it would end would be with one or all of their deaths.

Sarah ran to the bed. Clancy leapt onto the bed, reached under the pillow, pulled out a pistol, and stuck it in his belt. Sarah stomped her foot and went to the bureau.

Clancy smelled the bed and gagged. "Tell that man to take a bath!"

Clancy opened the window and arranged his flowers in a vase. A retired geisha once gave him Ikebana lessons, and he always looked for a chance to show off his skills.

"Sarah, my love, I am not going to say another word about that which is sitting at my place at our table–"

Clancy saw Sarah take a slug from the wine bottle she had pulled from the bureau. Clancy lunged and pulled the bottle out of her hands. Sarah pulled the pistol out of Clancy's belt and pointed it at him.

"If I get drunk," said Clancy, "people think I'm charming, but a drunken woman will have her children taken away and be sent to be cured. I know, it's not fair, but on the other hand, you get to stay at home with the twins. I have to go out with idiotic men and pretend to be interested in politics and sports!"

Clancy had tried to be a good husband. For four years, except for those two times with Mary, he was faithful to Sarah. He started courting Sarah – or rather, asked her to bed four minutes after first seeing her – after becoming aroused by the energetic way she hurled an onion at that cad who made sucking noises at her in the street: *now there's a woman who can fight her own duels!* he naively thought. The next time another man made an ungentlemanly remark, and Clancy said they should simply ignore a halfwit who appeared to have taken a bullet in the head during the French and Indian War, it was the end of any respect Sarah might have had for Clancy. Sarah would tolerate his presence as long as he put food on the table. And fixed the house. And bought her clothes. And bought new furniture. And gold jewelry. And and and and and and and and and and and and and and and and and and and and and and and and....

Clancy tried to put himself in Sarah's painful high-heeled shoes: *how lucky I was to be born a man. If I were a woman, they would have burned me for a witch by the time I was ten. If I was Sarah's height, constantly pushed around, judged only by my ever-fading beauty, I'd be just as angry.* But Clancy didn't know how to make up for all the other men in the world, other than killing every man who insulted her, charged her more, and made laws to suppress her. He'd have to slaughter half the population of Williamsburg and the entire House of Burgesses.

Clancy tried a new tactic. He grabbed Sarah's arm, yanked her so they were nose-to-nose and barked, "Pack your things, woman! We're going to Philadelphia!"

Sarah smiled and lowered the pistol. "Why can't you act like this all the time?"

"Because it's an act! I'm not going to pretend to be something I'm not in my own house!"

"I thought I was marrying Redbeard, not dickless Clancy."

Clancy let her go. Sarah held her hand out for the bottle. Clancy smashed the bottle on the floor. Sarah cocked the pistol and put it to Clancy's forehead.

"If you shoot me there, you'll hit empty air." Clancy pushed the pistol down to his chest.

Clancy gently took the pistol out of Sarah's shaking hand. Sarah grabbed onto the bureau to keep from falling over. Clancy wrapped his arms around Sarah and pressed his pelvis up against hers.

"Let's go to bed," Clancy whispered, "Forgive me. Give me another chance. I will do something, someday."

"Ha!" Sarah snorted.

Clancy let her go. "Then take the children and go to the Shawnee. Marry my cousin Hunting Bear. He loves women with guns. Terrible teeth, no sense of humor, but you'll never be cold or hungry. Promise me you'll go."

"To the Shawnee?" Sarah sneered. "It's the Indian in you that makes you an uncivilized monster."

Now Clancy was angry. "Au contraire, mon cher, it is the only civil part of me."

Sarah pulled another wine bottle from the bureau and uncorked it. As she lifted it to her lips, Clancy grabbed it and threw it out the window.

The iron-burned major, spoon frozen in mid-slurp, watched Clancy slam the bedroom door and storm out of the house. The major breathed a sigh of relief and opened his mouth to shovel more soup in, when Clancy marched back in and leaned across the table.

"As I have failed to satisfy my wife, I must yield to you, no matter how stinking, crass, uncultured, and pea-brained you may be…but, sir, if you even think of sending my children to England to be educated–"

Clancy pointed his pistol at the major's right eye.

"I went to an English school," Clancy said, "and look how I turned out."

Sarah opened the bedroom door, holding a rifle. Clancy dropped the pistol on the floor and raised his hands. Sarah aimed the rifle at Clancy. Clancy bolted. Sarah fired but, thanks to the wine she drank that morning, only managed to hit the oil lamp on the table. The iron-burned major dropped his spoon and screamed like a two-year-old.

KEEP WITHIN COMPASS.
FEAR GOD
BE SURE, TO AVOID MANY TROUBLES WHICH OTHERS ENDURE. KEEP WITHIN COMPASS AND YOU SHALL
INDUSTRY
PRODUCETH WEALTH

VII
CLANCY GETS HIMSELF TO A NUNNERY

lancy had to do something. Sarah was drinking again. She would bump her head against that low beam in the cellar, or fall down a staircase or into a well, be eaten by bears, or choke to death on a fishbone – not that Clancy ever dreamed that Sarah would magically vanish and free him from a tormented marriage so he could find true love and happiness – he had to get her away from that iron-burned redcoat who would pack his children off to England. How?

Clancy thought it was worth a try. And it was such a lovely walk through the woods. Clancy whistled the shanty *Farewell and Adieu* as he skipped down the dirt road.

There was only a small stone to mark the hidden path. Clancy leapt over the poison ivy and, making sure no one saw him, went into the woods, and found the crumbling house. The roof was solid; he had replaced it last spring. He stepped inside. Clancy saw five nuns, in their makeshift chapel, on their knees praying, illegally worshipping at their small altar. They looked so peaceful…it was too heavenly to bear –

"THIS IS A RAID!" Clancy screamed at the top of his lungs. "CONVERT – by order of the Church of England!"

The nuns screamed in holy terror, until they saw chuckling Clancy.

A bullet blew apart the holy water stoup. Clancy screamed. He screamed again when he saw Mother Superior standing in the doorway, pointing a rifle at him.

Clancy could not remember why he was ever interested in her. Oh, yes – his love of teaching. And sex. And teaching sex. When they met, she was a virgin. He thought he could help her learn to enjoy one of life's great pleasures. He was so unsuccessful, she became a nun. As Clancy waited for Mother Superior to finish her paperwork, his mind drifted to another woman, Mary, the woman he loved above all others.

Mary was by far the oldest prostitute in Williamsburg, having somehow avoided death by customer, disease, drink, or intentional overdose. Clancy could not believe his luck, to find such an intelligent, well-read woman close to his own age. At last: a woman to whom he didn't have to explain his jokes! Who never asked him "What were you thinking?!" (he usually wasn't) or "What are you thinking about?" (*At this particular moment? How nice it would be to have sex with another woman who didn't ask annoying questions.*) Why did he ever waste time on young girls? Why didn't he pay heed to the letter Dr. Franklin sent him in '45, listing the benefits of taking an older mistress?

So many years wasted dealing with high drama and immaturity.

As they went upstairs for their first encounter, Clancy noticed Mary was exhausted. He suggested they meet the next day, after she'd had a nice rest. He handed her a coin: "For you, madam, I would wait a week," he smiled, and kissed her hand. Mary could not believe his chivalry and consideration, especially after the stories she'd heard about the Redbeards.

The next day, clean-shaven but bleary-eyed Clancy said, "Madam, yesterday I insulted you. For you, I would wait a year." When he had kissed her hand, Clancy saw her gnarled fingers. He spent all night crafting a pole with a trigger at one end, and a wire running down to a set of claws at the other. Even with her crippled hand, Mary could easily squeeze the trigger and pick objects off floors and shelves or use it on obnoxious clients. Clancy also brought her a copy of his favorite play, *The Jew of Malta*. He thought it was hilarious, pointing out the hypocrisies of man's invented religions. And he brought biscuits. Mary never had such a thoughtful customer. They went upstairs and Clancy was so aroused he lasted about four seconds, and then they ate the biscuits and played with Clancy's invention, which, he said, in the tradition of Dr. Franklin, he would not patent, but present to all who needed it. Clancy told her about his many failings that he was deeply ashamed of but didn't know how to fix, and how everything he did from the moment he woke in the morning until he fell asleep at night was to impress women so they'd have sex with him, or to earn money so women would be impressed and have sex with him, and while a few women might have temporarily enjoyed his company, there was really no reason why he should have been born, let alone been given fifty years when far better man were given only thirty, and how he longed to really do something. Clancy knew with her help and understanding heart, it would be easy to become a better man. Who needed the Freemasons when you had Mary? To show his gratitude, Clancy spread Mary's legs and showed her some virtuosic tonguing he mastered in France. If all men were like Clancy, Mary thought, she might look forward to going to work.

It was wonderful to talk with a woman with a mind of her own. The most beautiful young girl Clancy ever courted became repulsive with her continuous chorus of *Yes, Clancy, yes, YES!* and not just in the bedroom. Clancy knew he couldn't possibly be right all the time. How was he going to become a better man, if a woman didn't occasionally kick his ass?

The only bump on Mary's road was when Clancy remembered his vow, before embarking on his latest Rescue That Wench mission, to ask the woman if she required rescuing. So, he asked Mary if she enjoyed working as a prostitute. "What? OF COURSE NOT!" she snapped. (*Well, your colleague Nancy does!* She said she would never marry Clancy because she enjoyed sleeping with many, many men, and having legal control of her own money. Clancy decided to leave Nancy out of the conversation. Her name might never come up, unless he accidentally called it out during orgasm. Clancy had practiced moaning *Mary, Mary…Mary, Mary, Mary….*)

A week later, Clancy asked Mary, on bended knee, if she would agree to retire and marry him. He said he loved her and would be proud to be seen anywhere with such a refined, intelligent woman, but presumed it would be annoying for her to stay and endure rude comments from closed-minded Williamsburgers – so where would she like to live? As they would live off his income as a musician, it needed to be in a large metropolis. Philadelphia was his choice. Boston was too puritanical for his tastes. New York? He liked the idea of living surrounded by water, but it was too expensive, too materialist, too in love with royalty. But wherever they lived, it must be near the sea.

Later that afternoon, Clancy learned that Sarah, bedridden at her parents' house with what they had prayed was an enormous stomach tumor, had that morning given birth to red-haired twins. Clancy told Sarah yes, of course he would accept responsibility, and to keep the innocent little dears from being called The Bastards of the Bastard of Redbeard for the rest of their lives, he and Sarah would marry that evening…and he wept as he walked up Duke of Gloucester Street to tell Mary the news. Mary handed *The Jew of Malta* back to Clancy and said if he had been trying to hint that she was like the character of Bellamira, the gold-hungry scheming courtesan, not to worry: if she wanted to shake down a man, she'd pick someone with better prospects than The Bastard of Redbeard, and she went back to reading *Tristram Shandy*, a gift from young, rich Tom Jefferson. Clancy, who had prayed Mary would break his skull with his pick-up device and put him out of his forthcoming misery, cried all the way down Duke of Gloucester Street to Sarah and his hideous future in-laws.

Mother Superior sat at her mold-covered desk, writing with more zeal than Rafe Naider. Clancy stood next to her like a disobedient schoolboy waiting for his hand to be whipped. She was the oldest twenty-seven-year-old woman he'd ever seen. He wished he hadn't broken Sarah's last bottle. He could really use a drink now, to steady his nerves. Clancy realized this was the first time he ever faced Mother Superior sober.

Mother Superior jabbed her quill in her inkwell. "You're a disgrace. You had the best education. You had money, strength, health, height – and you pissed it all away."

"Mother Superior, Sarah has taken to drink again and is with an unmusical redcoat. I beg you, take her in."

"She is a weak woman."

"I drove her to it! Please, do not punish her for my stupidity." Clancy dropped to his knees and clutched her hem. "Polly…if I had known my antics would drive you into a nunnery… I'm sorry for the appalling way I behaved. I was bored. A musician in a small town…if only we'd moved to Philadelphia! You could have become a Druid and no one there would have blinked an eye. Please, Polly, take Sarah and my children in."

Polly kept writing. "Everywhere you go, you leave a trail of wreckage. You've spent your whole life financing your weaknesses: gambling, wine, women…you kill everything you touch."

"For the sake of your fellow woman, help Mary."

"That 'woman' is a whore."

"What choice of profession did she have? When she resisted her brother's advances, he broke her fingers. She can't do any handiwork."

"I had the same start in life as those women, and I did not lower myself to such depths."

"Because you had a man's money; *my* money."

Polly – Mother Superior – glared at him. Damn it, he shouldn't have said that – but after cruelty, Clancy most hated hypocrisy. "I beg you, help Sarah."

"Any woman stupid enough to marry you deserves what she gets. I've been punished; now it's her turn."

Clancy dropped her hem. "In all these years you've been God's lover, have you not grown a heart, you cold bitch?"

Clancy was glad to have things out. Any affection he once had for her vanished, and he was free of her at last. He had married her in the wake of the death of Patrick, his eldest son. Clancy swore to himself that if he ever thought of attempting to tie Henry VIII's marriage record (the sheer number, not the beheadings), he would wait until he was sober, have a six-month engagement, and talk with the woman for two hours every day – *while sober*. And he would pick a woman past childbearing age, so there would be no collateral damage when the relationship exploded.

Clancy got off his knees, kicking up the dirt floor.

"Where is the floor?" he demanded.

"The what?"

"The marble floor I spent an eternity working for, so you wouldn't have to live like a pig!"

"I did not want anything that was obtained by playing the devil's music."

Clancy asked, "Then, pray tell, who did?"

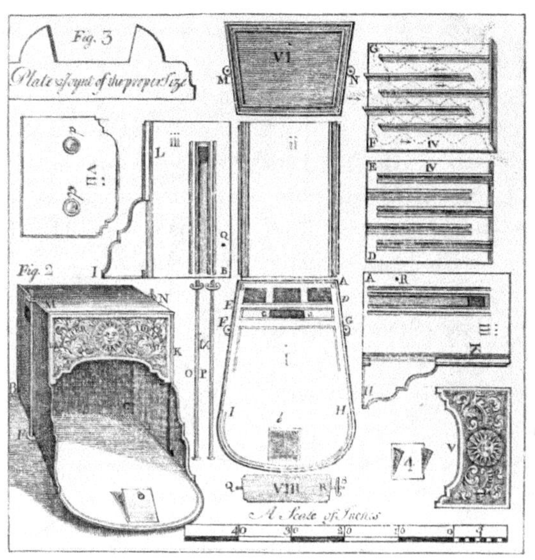

VIII
CLANCY BEATS UP A PRIEST

Clancy kicked open the Reverend's front door and let his crowbar bang on the marble floor to announce his arrival. The house was behind Bruton Parish, Church of England, that bastion of moral authority, which Henry the Eighth invented so he could divorce the first of his six wives.

As Clancy employed his crowbar to take back his marble floor, he looked up and saw The Reverend Harrison – the clergyman at his hanging – sitting at the dining table, a chicken drumstick in his mouth.

As the Reverend choked on his chicken, Clancy walked up

to the table and examined the china plates rimmed in gold, the crystal glasses, the silver goblets, the silver engraved candle holders, the gold engraved dessert caddy filled with cocoa nuts...

The Reverend waved the drumstick as though swatting at a fly. "Heretic! Heathen! Be gone!"

Clancy slipped the silverware into his bag. He grabbed a handful of cocoa nuts, pocketed them, and jumped onto the Reverend's table. The Reverend bolted up and backed against the wall. Clancy jumped down from the table, planted himself in the Reverend's chair, and dug into his dinner. The Reverend hit Clancy on the head with the drumstick.

Clancy said, "Listen, priest–"

"I am The Reverend Harrison! I am the Church of England!"

Clancy snorted. "How would it be, if I told the good people of Williamsburg, you were, until you landed on these shores a few years ago, Father O'Flannagan?"

"You wouldn't dare, Bastard of Redbeard."

"The only reason I'm not exposing you, Catholic boy," Clancy said between bites of the Reverend's dinner, "is to protect Polly and the sisters."

"Sinner. Confess your sins!"

"Confess? I could not keep my hands off my employers' wives...and daughters...and mothers..."

"You little fiend!" The Reverend slapped Clancy's hair.

"I was a disappointment to my Indian mother."

"Savage!"

"Sometimes, I was so caught up in my own pleasure, I failed to bring my women to a climax," Clancy said, looking at the Reverend, slowly licking his plate with the tip of his tongue.

The Reverend was so aghast, only a little squeak escaped from his gaping mouth.

"I have been sexually unfaithful to women, but never unfaithful to myself. Mental infidelity is professing to believe what one does not, Father O'Flannagan. When a man corrupts and prostitutes the chastity of his mind, he prepares himself for the commission of every other crime. The priest becomes the Reverend for a marble floor. Churches are human inventions, devised to terrify and enslave mankind, and to monopolize power and profit. I think Rafe Naider and Captain Death are closer to God than you will ever be."

Clancy tossed the plate into the fireplace and picked up the wine goblet. "I do not acknowledge any authority claimed by the Church of England, the Catholic Church, the Protestant church, nor any other invented religious entity. My church is my own mind."

The Reverend covered his ears and screamed, feeling he had entered hell and was being engulfed by flames. And then he looked down and realized he had stepped into the fireplace.

On a side table, Clancy saw a voluptuous, uncut watermelon. He sauntered towards it.

"Oh, that's better than pie," Clancy said softly as he caressed the melon's smooth skin. The Reverend had no wife nor daughter to take: this beauty would have to do. Clancy pulled out his sgian-dubh, plunged it into the melon, twisted it, pulled it out, and unbuttoned his breeches. The Reverend almost passed out. He closed his eyes and stuck his fingers in his ears as Clancy mounted and penetrated the melon's succulent red flesh.

"This won't take long," Clancy promised as he thrust. "It never – oh, ahhhhh…*Mary, Mary*…" The ravished melon fell off the table and rolled across the room, leaving a sticky white trail that the Reverend prayed the servants would mistake for meringue.

Clancy buttoned himself back up and wondered if having relations with a melon constituted being unfaithful to Sarah. During their marriage, he had been on intimate terms mostly with own hands (being ambidextrous came in handy). Clancy downed half the wine and tossed the remains into the fireplace. The wine nourished the flames, which licked out and set the Reverend's hem on fire. The screaming Reverend rolled on Clancy's marble floor and extinguished the fire. Clancy sighed. Had the Reverend gone up in flames, his demise might be ruled

Death by Spontaneous Combustion. Now, Clancy would have to forever watch his back.

The Reverend pulled a crucifix from under his shirt. He ripped it off its chain and held it upside down like a sword. Clancy picked up a fork from the table and assumed a dueling position. With his free left hand, Clancy slapped the Reverend across the face. The Reverend grabbed his injured face, and Clancy snatched the crucifix and pulled the figure of Jesus off the cross.

"Leave Him out of this," said Clancy, gently tucking Jesus into his pocket. Clancy liked Jesus and hated seeing him being tortured. *Bloody Catholics. Did they ever make jewelry with uplifting images of Jesus feeding the poor, healing the sick, driving the moneychangers from the temple, or installing Franklin Rods? Nooooo, they must scare everyone into unquestioning docility with the threat of an excruciating death.* Clancy handed the crucifix back to the Reverend, and they resumed dueling stances. Clancy switched the fork from his right hand to his left, confusing the Reverend to no end. What man uses his left hand equally as well as his right? What devil was he facing? With his right hand, Clancy slapped the Reverend across the face. As the Reverend grabbed his injured cheek, Clancy snatched the crucifix and tossed it into the fire. The Reverend screamed and ran to the fire, tried to pull the crucifix out, and screamed as he burned his hand.

Clancy sat at the table and ate two oysters. The Reverend pulled Clancy's ear. Clancy pushed his chair back, bent down, grabbed the Reverend's robe's hem, and yanked it up and over the Reverend's head.

"UNHAND ME! AGH!"

Clancy reached between the Reverend's legs. The Reverend let out high-pitched shrieks and screams. Uncertain if the Reverend was squealing in pain or pleasure, Clancy worked fast, lest it was the latter; the Reverend was often seen being overly friendly to the little boys in Williamsburg. Clancy pulled the purse from under the Reverend's robes, and the Reverend's *Yes! YES!* quickly descended into *No! NO!* Blinded by fabric, The Reverend ran into a wall. Clancy opened the Reverend's purse and admired the English coins, not as pretty as Spanish coins, but they would do. The Reverend pulled his robe back down. As Clancy walked to the front door, the Reverend lunged at him with an oyster knife. Clancy grabbed the Reverend by his collar, spun him around as though he were a discus, and hurled the Reverend into a wall, knocking him out cold.

Clancy knew he should take the money straight home, bash the iron-burned redcoat's head into the Franklin stove, bark at Sarah and drag her to Philadelphia…

…but Clancy really needed a new suit. A nice suit would facilitate their journey, eliciting invitations to dinners and free lodgings – *think of the savings!*

The tailors were thrilled to see him. They loved makeovers. And Clancy paid in English coin. How did he get them? It was illegal to export coin from England, so as not to debase the currency. Best not to ask… Clancy took Jesus out of his pocket and the tailors threw his borrowed coat into the fire, *crackle, crackle.* Thanks to Clancy lending his two hands, they had it ready before sunset. Tom Jefferson's half-finished suit lay in the back room, and now that his credit was shakier than ever, well…just add a little fabric to the back seams… Clancy stripped off his old breeches, and the tailors screamed and hurled themselves against the far wall when they saw black spots on Clancy's penis. They were relieved when Clancy easily peeled off the watermelon seeds.

Clancy tucked Jesus into his new coat pocket, threw open the door, called "THAAAAANKK YOOOOOOOOOOU!" so everyone in Williamsburg could hear, and marched down the steps wearing a cocked hat, purple velvet coat and silk breeches, red stockings, and gold buckled shoes. He stuck a feather in his hat, the perfect macaroni. The sun, low on the horizon, shone on his glory. A woman walking stopped and curtseyed. Clancy doffed his hat. Two tradesmen passing by stopped and bowed.

Mr. Dandridge, the eighty-year-old gentleman who had recognized Raider Kelvin at the King's Arms Tavern, rode past in his carriage. Dandridge knew if he stopped drinking so much, these hallucinations would go away…but what a wonderful hallucination! His childhood hero, in the flesh! Dandridge pounded the carriage's ceiling with his walking stick and his coachman brought his team to a stop.

Dandridge hopped out of the carriage and hobbled to Clancy. "I'm seeing a ghost! Redbeard! It can't be! You must be his reincarnation!"

"Clancy Redbeard, at your service."

"You're on your way to your brother's party, of course?"

Dandridge begged Clancy to accept a ride with him. Clancy smiled and stepped into the carriage.

IX
AUNT ANNE BONNY

Alas, Mr. Dandridge's wife was also in the carriage. She glared at Clancy the entire journey. Mr. Dandridge looked at Clancy and, like most people, saw the ghost of Redbeard. Dandridge sighed, "How I miss your father. I am surprised I never ran into more Redbeard sons. There must be a thousand of you!"

"Nay," said Clancy, "only two." The Redbeard bloodline was dying. Only the most recent of his brother Roderick's seven wives had produced offspring, a girl and boy, whom Clancy had never met, and whom he knew were not his brother's. Why couldn't men admit they were firing blank rounds and stop pointing their penises at their "barren" wives?

Of Clancy's children, only three remained: Sarah's twins, and his daughter in Scotland – plus the bonus black boy with oriental eyes, whom he was happy to give support and his name but knew wasn't, from a scientific standpoint, his.

"But…Angus?" asked Dandridge.

"Killed by the Pamunkey." Clancy always wondered what Angus did to so enrage that peaceful tribe that they took a day off from their farming to dig a deep hole, cover it with branches, and lure Angus to his death. Whatever it was, Clancy was sure Angus deserved it.

"And Nicol, and Gordon?"

"Like my other twenty-three half-brothers, all killed in the French and Indian War." It was a lie, but it sounded good and would end this line of questioning. Nicol was shot in a duel over a woman, lingered for three months, and was finished off by a bee sting; Gordon got drunk, fell out of a ground floor window at Chowning's Tavern, landed head-first in a horse trough and drowned. Most of Clancy's half-brothers died ridiculous deaths from idiotic acts of bravado, trying to imitate Father – like Finlay, who stole chocolate from a little girl, who then killed him with her slingshot. Clancy always longed to find that now twenty-year-old girl and marry her: *now that's the kind of woman with whom you want to go to war!*

Dandridge's uppity wife glared at Clancy and proclaimed, "It's God's will."

Clancy wanted to strike her, but his cravat was so tight, he thought if he leaned forward, he would be strangled. Clancy looked out the carriage window at the approaching mansion and plantation.

Clancy jumped out of the carriage, and ran past the party guests, the bewigged slaves and indentured servants, and up the ornately carved staircase, past the hundred rifles, pistols and swords displayed on the walls as a none-too-subtle hint to visitors. The butler dropped a tray of wine glasses when he saw Clancy, remembering his last visit.

In the Great Hall, guests saw Clancy and parted like the Red Sea. As the host turned around, Clancy threw his arms around him and hugged him with all his might.

"Brother…" said Clancy.

Because all of Virginia's gentry was staring at him, Roderick managed a benevolent half-smile, and a few feeble slaps on Clancy's back, "There, there." Roderick turned Clancy around by the shoulders and introduced him.

"May I present Clancy, one of Father's little mistakes."

The twenty guests ate sweet potato pudding, Clancy in the last seat at the end, Roderick at the head of the table flanked by portraits of Queen Charlotte and King George III.

"Rafe Naider and his Raiders are a bigger menace than Captain Death," Roderick told his guests. "Naider claims to be law-abiding, but his speeches are fanning the flames more than the Sons of Liberty. Naider should be extradited to England and tried for treason…."

An ethereal note wafted in the air. The guests glanced around the room for the source. They'd heard the mansion was haunted by Roderick's last wife, whose sudden death was never explained.

Clancy absentmindedly played an *F* on his wine glass. He had never wanted a drink so much in his life, but knew he had better stay on his toes around Roderick. Clancy looked up, saw the guests looking at him, and stopped playing.

"Forgive me. Occupational hazard."

A red-nosed man asked, "Do you own a glass factory, Captain Redbeard?"

"*Captain*?" Roderick sneered. "I think when one gets drunk and rams one's ship into London Bridge, one loses one's command. Clancy plays musical glasses in the streets."

The guests gasped. Clancy wished he could boast about how much money he earned as a pathetic street musician. But he also wished to leave Roderick's house alive. Clancy needed to keep Roderick feeling that Clancy was so far beneath him, he was no threat. And that Clancy had earned all his money was not impressive. The other guests had made their money the respectable way: they inherited it.

"Playing in the streets…" mumbled the old woman sitting across from Clancy.

Clancy looked at the seventy-four-year-old woman who sat opposite him, pickled in brandy, her chin resting on her chest, and gasped.

"Aunt Anne!"

Clancy hadn't seen her in over twenty years, and this was the last place he expected to see Mad Aunt Anne. Why was Roderick keeping her? She had to be serving some purpose. Was she minding his children?

The guests seated across from Clancy looked at him, and then up at the painting hanging on the wall behind Clancy. The portrait resembled Clancy, painted in a primitive style. A tipsy woman asked Roderick, "Is that your brother's self-portrait?"

Roderick flinched at *your brother.* "No, that's Father, painted by *my* mother."

Mad Aunt Anne stood, knocking her chair over. "Do you want to see a truly fine painting? A masterpiece?" she asked the guests.

"No, Aunt Anne," said Clancy before Roderick could.

"I'll show you…" and Mad Aunt Anne ran out. Roderick glared at the servants, and they ran after her. Roderick kicked himself for not sending Mad Aunt Anne to the waters at Berkeley, where her tales would be written off as madness and not autobiography. It did not look good for a man to live alone on a such a large estate, without a single relation, and he had few from which to choose. Aunt Anne sufficed, if she kept to the small cottage a mile away from the mansion's firearms.

From the corridor, Mad Aunt Anne shouted, "You look at this…this…"

Mad Aunt Anne came back through the other door, evading the servants, hoisting a four-by-six-foot portrait. She dropped it onto the table. It was a masterpiece of an old man resembling Clancy.

"Little Bastard Clancy painted this when he was fourteen

years old," said Mad Aunt Anne. "Painted it in a gale — the steadiest hand on the seven seas."

The guests smiled at Clancy, with a new respect, and silently vowed to hire him to paint their portraits. He was far more talented than that John Singleton Copley, and Clancy would not make them pose with a squirrel or rodent or other animal that might defecate on their best furniture. Better yet, for all his flaws, Clancy was not a Bostonian.

Clancy said, "Aunt Anne, tell us the story about how our father and Blackbeard set their beards on fire."

"My, my, look at the time, Aunt–" Roderick said, and two servants took Aunt Anne's arms, lifted her up, and carried her out.

Clancy added, "Or the story of how the Royal Governor grew tired of chasing Father around Chesapeake Bay and hired him to kill every Iroquois in Virginia."

"Goodnight, Aunt Anne," called Roderick.

Roderick's brown-nosed associate raised his glass: "A toast: to Redbeard, who rid Virginia of the Indian menace."

"Here, here!" said the guests.

Clancy attempted to leave, but the other guests kept blocking his path. Mr. Dandridge poked Clancy in the ribs. "If you grow tired of playing in the street for pennies, in my business ventures, I'm always in need of a good pirate."

"I'm afraid I am legitimate," Clancy said.

"Legitimate is the last thing you are," Dandridge's wife sneered as she left.

As the last couple walked out, the front doors slammed, and two servants blocked Clancy's exit. Clancy turned and saw a guard standing at every doorway, in front of every window, and blocking the staircase.

Roderick's lemon-faced secretary pointed to the library. Clancy gulped. He took one step toward the front door. All the guards took one step towards Clancy.

"Your brother is waiting," said the secretary.

"I would like to say goodnight to my Aunt Anne…"

Clancy took one step toward the staircase. The guards all took one more step towards Clancy, their hands on their sidearms.

Clancy went into the library. Roderick sat at his desk, signing papers. The secretary gestured for Clancy to sit opposite Roderick. The secretary stood in the corner. When a log in the fireplace crackled, Clancy jumped. Roderick put his papers to the side, poured a glass of wine, and pushed it in front of Clancy. Roderick did not pour a glass for himself.

Clancy pondered, *why on earth did I come here? Damn this new suit!* He thought if Roderick saw it, and saw how the other guests respected him…*what was I thinking? I could design a more efficient slave ship that would make Roderick even richer, win the Copley medal, and marry the wealthiest woman in Virginia, and Roderick would still hate me. He would hate me more: how dare I show him up…!* Clancy leaned forward, away from the back of the chair, in case his brother's secretary came up behind him and attempted to strangle him – a few extra inches might buy him enough time to dodge the garrote.

Roderick smiled. "Why do you not visit more often? You live only five miles hence, but I have not seen you in years!" Roderick's sudden bursts of friendliness always frightened Clancy.

"Well," Clancy said gingerly, "after my last visit, when you said, 'If you ever step foot in my house again, I'll have you hanged, drawn and quartered,' I decided that another visit was probably unwise. I did send for you, when I was in thrown in jail."

Roderick said. "I have a job for you! I am very interested in aiding Rafe Naider, but he's a difficult man to find."

Clancy blinked. "But…at supper–"

"One has to say certain things to one's less enlightened business associates."

Clancy was distracted by the portrait of Roderick's deceased wife on the far wall. "I would like to meet your children."

"You must come for Christmas," Roderick said. "Governor Dunmore is coming, and you can show off your carving skills."

"Are we going to eat him?" Clancy quipped, then quickly wiped the grin off his face.

Roderick leaned forward. "Naider is bound for Savannah?" Clancy looked down.

Roderick said, "Get aboard the *JUSTICE* as soon as you can, and report back when they land...in Boston."

Roderick smiled and poured himself a glass of wine.

"I would like to meet my nephew and niece," said Clancy. "Are they upstairs?"

"At school – home at Christmas. A toast: to *JUSTICE*."

Clancy picked up his glass but waited for Roderick to drink first. He did pour from the same bottle, but that secretary could have lined Clancy's glass with poison. If Roderick was after him again, Clancy didn't want to go on living. The last time Roderick got it in his mind to do away with him, when Clancy dared to correct Roderick's misuse of some naval terminology at a party, it was twelve years of looking over his shoulder, never the same tavern two nights in a row, and never taking a wife for fear she, and her family, and her friends, would be marked. It wasn't until Roderick shifted his attention to doing away with his other half-brothers – the two who dared to start a rival slave transport company – that Clancy was off the hook. Now, no siblings stood between Roderick and Clancy.

Clancy downed the wine and choked. When he realized it wasn't poisoned, just a horrible local vintage, he laughed. Roderick glared at him. Insulting Roderick's choice of wine would be justification for assassination in Roderick's book.

Clancy said, between coughs, "I thought...I thought when you called me in here...you were going to have me killed."

It took Roderick two full seconds to start laughing.

X

GEORGE WASHINGTON'S
MUSICAL GLASSES

aving escaped Roderick's mansion – Clancy's mansion, but that was another story – Clancy needed a stiff drink before he did something. He had no intention of leading Roderick's men to Naider so they could sink *JUSTICE*. Clancy would head south. Perhaps Captain Death was alive in South Carolina, waiting for Clancy to break him out of jail. Clancy could help him raid Edward Rutledge's plantation, and use the

71

money to get Sarah and Mad Aunt Anne to a spa, get them sober…

Clancy went to the Raleigh Tavern, got in thanks to his new suit, asked to see Mary, and was told she had gone away with a widowed man who had money and two children. Clancy breathed a sigh of relief. He hoped the widower would treat Mary better than he had. And then he started to cry, knowing he would most likely never see her again. The tavern keeper told Clancy his crying was killing business and kicked him out. Clancy needed something stronger than alcohol. He walked to the Edinburgh Castle Tavern and drowned his sorrow in chocolate.

All the men were discussing politics and sports. Clancy was starved for female company, even if it didn't lead to a bedroom. He regretted he had no sisters. He wondered if he would love all women so much had he been exposed to them twenty-four hours a day as a child. He might have joined the Royal Navy simply to get away from them. "I only have sons," boasted Father Redbeard at one party after the other. After hearing it for the nine-hundredth time, Clancy quipped, "Hardly an accomplishment to be proud of," and it was back to the cellar for The Bastard of Redbeard.

Clancy may have had sisters. He heard tales of girls being given away, sold, and drowned. "Sons of pirates come in handy, but daughters?" laughed his father. Clancy had asked, "Why not employ them as spies?" The kind of work Clancy's father thought suitable for women, well, perhaps it was best if they met an early demise. Clancy constantly worried that he might unknowingly sleep with one of his half-sisters. He avoided redheads and always asked women about their families. If a woman couldn't readily identify her father, Clancy usually could not rise to the occasion.

Clancy sat alone, wiping chocolate off his nose. Through the open window, Clancy saw William Lee, a former jockey, now a manservant, who two years previously gave Clancy a tip that his master's horse was about to go lame, and Clancy won twenty pounds racing the colonel around the College of

William & Mary riding on a jackass. Clancy wondered what the colonel did to make Mr. Lee turn on his master like that…perhaps, not giving him his freedom? Clancy picked up his chocolate, stood, and was about to go out and sit with the engaging and loquacious Mr. Lee, when every man turned and looked at Clancy; what was this gentleman doing, standing with a cup of chocolate?

Clancy shook his ass as though it had fallen asleep and sat back down. *Must have traveled over rough roads, carriage springs must need replacing,* and the men went back to discussing politics and sports. In bad weather, Clancy needed odd jobs, and if anyone saw him socializing with a slave… Clancy handed the server a coin and asked him to take a cup of chocolate and a pie out to Mr. Lee. "Who's Mr. Lee? You mean, *Billy?*" The server said he would, but sneered, "MISTER Lee…!" Clancy wanted to kick the server in the breeches. Blacks, even free ones, had it bad; was the server so small he had to kick them? Clancy got so angry he banged his cup down and splashed chocolate on his breeches, making it look like he had shat them. The day had started out rotten and gotten worse and worse…he should have gone with Kelvin! Clancy hated playing Gentleman. *Damn this suit. Why did I let those snobbish tailors burn that perfectly good suit? Apart from a bullet hole in the chest, it was fine! To hell with it, I'm going to see Mary* – and then he remembered she was gone. Clancy was on the verge of cracking up –

Mr. Lee's master, Colonel George Washington, elegantly dressed as always, entered with the more soberly dressed Patrick Henry. Clancy would have stood, but if they saw those brown stains… "I see you're a traveling man, Colonel Washington!" Clancy sang out. Henry was not a Freemason, so Clancy did not include him in his special greeting. "And Mr. Henry, welcome back to Devilsburg." Clancy gestured for them to sit with him. "I hope you gentlemen had fun with your fellow burgesses in your extralegal session at the Raleigh, deciding the fate of the common man."

"Thank you, sir," said Washington, alarmed that the gentleman knew about their clandestine meeting, but presumed, from his friendliness, he approved of it. "And with whom do we have the pleasure of drinking chocolate tonight?"

Clancy thought Washington must have been drinking heavily at the Raleigh. He didn't recognize Clancy? What an opportunity! He could pretend to be a visitor from the backwoods, challenge Washington to a game of cards, and win enough to buy a carriage for Sarah and the twins.

Alas, Patrick Henry always saw through everything: "The Glass Musician of Williamsburg!"

Clancy bowed while seated, arms out, showing off his embroidered sleeves and lace cuffs. "I have reclaimed my stolen fortune and retired."

"Well played," Henry said. "I always suspected you were a gentleman."

"But a pity for me," said Washington. "At Mount Vernon, we have a device that no one can figure out how to play...it's made from glass bowls."

Clancy choked. Chocolate shot out his nose.

"Benjamin Franklin's armonica?!"

Clancy accepted Washington's invitation to stay at his home in Fairfax County, though he wondered about the colonel's ulterior motives. Perhaps Washington just wanted to go foxhunting or hoped to get back at him for winning that horse/jackass race. If he let the colonel win every race and card game, Clancy felt confident Washington would employ him. Clancy would send for Sarah and the twins (*adieu, iron-burned redcoat!*) and they'd all have a grand adventure as Clancy surveyed for the colonel. He could tolerate being far from the sea for a short time. Sarah and the twins would stay in good taverns: he would be Washington's Man, they'd be treated well. They would work their way north, settle in Philadelphia, and Clancy would play Washington's armonica not on the streets but in warm salons, dazzling Philadelphians with Dr. Franklin's invention. Any heavy drinker could scavenge together a set of musical wine glasses, if they were chummy with enough tavern proprietresses, but only the wealthiest men could afford a glass armonica. People would finally treat him with some respect.

Clancy asked if Washington's mother would be at Mount Vernon? "NO!" Washington said louder than he intended. When Clancy breathed a sigh of relief, so did Washington, and the two men grew closer on the journey. Mary Ball Washington terrified Clancy. She was just like the colonel but smarter, and a better equestrian and card player. She would send Clancy home penniless and barefoot. Washington was still bitter that his mother had refused to let him leave home to attend Appleby Grammar School in England or join the Royal Navy. Clancy told Washington the fates had other plans for him, and he was sure all would work out in his favor. Washington liked Clancy. Clancy was a Freemason, and the fourth best horseman in Virginia, after Mother, himself, and William Lee. Finally, a white man who could keep up with him. Or probably white. There were rumors about the mother. *What was Clancy's family name?* Washington had always been too busy thinking about himself to overhear much gossip about Clancy, one of the few white men in Virginia routinely called by his Christian name — if he was white (he may have just been tanned), and if he was a Christian (Washington never saw Clancy at Burton Parish). Only slaves, indentured servants, and horses were called by their first names: even children were *Mister* or *Miss.* Washington felt perturbed any time he saw Clancy around Williamsburg, as though he had seen him long, long ago...

Clancy rode with Mr. Lee, Washington, and Patrick Henry through the countryside. Washington pointed to his horse's disintegrating bridle and roared, "It arrived three weeks ago, and look at it! Look at this 'English craftsmanship!' Rafe Naider needs to prosecute the merchants who sell us this rubbish."

"But, colonel," Clancy said, surprised that Washington

seemed surprised, "Virginia and the other territories were colonized for one purpose: to export our wealth to England…well, that, and to dump second sons, ugly daughters, bastards, scandalous women, convicts, and the Scots and Irish. What should we expect when we have hereditary succession? A king, and a House of Lords, in this day and age? Why was Parliament created but to give the masses the appearance of representation, and to benefit a handful of merchants? Yes, we can petition, but did pleading with one's master, *oh, please, sir, do not whip me!* ever do anything but make the master whip harder, to show who's in charge?"

Washington and Henry looked at Clancy, agog.

Henry finally said, "What were you doing playing music on street corners? Why were you not a lawyer?"

Washington asked, projecting his own restlessness onto Clancy, "Would you be able to sit still at a desk for the required two years of study with Mr. Wythe?"

Henry sniffed. "Two years? I read for six weeks! Now that you're retired, Clancy, and have someone else looking after your family, you could do it in five! I'd be happy to sign your license, provided, of course, that you agree to serve as my clerk for three or four years…"

How did he know about the redcoat in my house? Clancy wondered. News spreads fast in Devilsburg.

Clancy said, "Mr. Henry, you and Rafe Naider must join forces, and tear these parliamentary criminals apart in court!"

"Sir, I do not collaborate with outlaws."

"Outlaws? You think Rafe Naider capable of breaking a law?"

Washington said, "I doubt Mr. Henry would associate with such a heathen."

"I don't know what Naider believes, and I don't care!" said Clancy. "He does God's work on earth. Isn't that enough?"

Henry proclaimed: "I'd sooner join with Captain Death."

When they reached Hanover County, Patrick Henry broke off to ride home to Scotchtown. Clancy longed to stop and visit Mrs. Henry, ill since the birth of her sixth child, and rumored to be kept in a straitdress in the cellar (and wouldn't a sixth child drive any mother insane?), but "gentlemen" did not do such things, *damn "propriety" and this suit!*

Clancy, Mr. Lee, and Washington proceeded north to the Potomac River and the mansion at the grandest of Washington's five farms, Mount Vernon. A lightning rod had recently been installed. Clancy couldn't wait to see the other Franklin goodie Washington had procured.

While Colonel Washington raged at his overseer about how his mansion had gone to hell in his absence, Clancy "borrowed" a pair of the colonel's clean breeches.

A slave opened the dining room door for Clancy and Washington. All the walls and moldings were painted in the latest fashionable color, which made Clancy seasick, something no ocean could do. He barely suppressed his vomit reflex.

"Ah…*verdigris green*…" Clancy staggered…

…and then he saw the glass armonica.

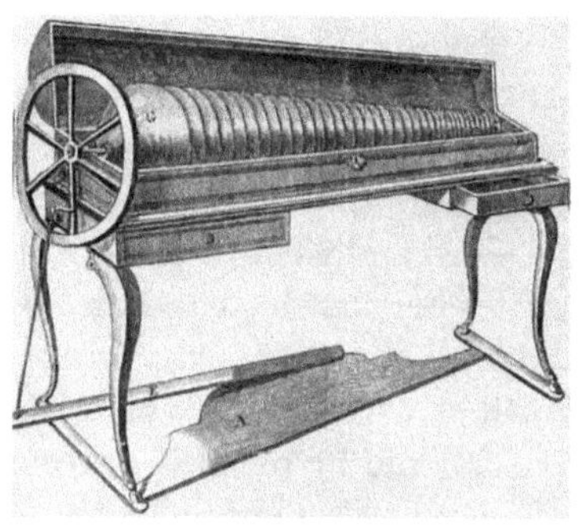

"Ohhhhh…Benjamin Franklin, our great creator."

"In the presence of more fervently devout persons, you may wish to say *inventor*," Washington suggested.

"When people hear this, they may think Dr. Franklin is the Almighty."

Clancy took flowers out of a vase and dipped his fingers in

the vase water. Clancy engaged the foot pedal, and the thirty-seven horizontally mounted glass bowls spun. Clancy played the first two bars of *God Save the King*.

"Not that!" Washington ordered.

Clancy grinned. He played *Chester* by William Billings. The door opened. Washington looked over. When Clancy finished, he looked up.

Martha Washington stood in the doorway, tears pouring down her chubby red cheeks.

"You were sent by heaven," said Mrs. Washington.

"Most women would say the other place," Clancy winked at her, and used his Ikebana skills to rearrange the flowers.

rs. Washington kept sneaking little glimpses of Mr. Clancy out of the corner of her eye, trying to remember where she first saw him, and why her heart was pounding. She was quite certain he had once proposed to her. That narrowed it down to one hundred sixty-five men. She did not remember it was at a party eighteen years earlier, when Clancy was less beaten by weather and life, and his hair so flaming red it burned her retinas. She was then Martha Dandridge, age seventeen and scouting potential husbands. Society told Clancy he was finished mourning his first wife, but he was still devastated from losing her, and not ready to risk inflicting death on another woman. Clancy left the party without saying a word and went to sea.

Years later, after her first husband died, Clancy missed his second opportunity to marry Martha when he was jailed for lechery. It was just as well: Clancy would have felt even more impotent than usual, had he married a woman with far more money than he (Colonel Washington had no such qualms). No, it would have never worked. Martha owned three hundred slaves. Clancy would have moved the slaves into the house and waited upon them. Clancy, unlike most men, took the Golden Rule seriously. It would have turned Virginia upside down.

Clancy liked his women with a wee bit of extra meat on them, something to hang onto, but Martha was beginning to look like one of his father-in-law's farmed hogs, and Clancy didn't think he'd ever earn enough to feed a woman this ravenous. He'd have to turn her loose to forage in the forest. Yes, everything had worked out in the end…except for Clancy being stuck in a loveless marriage, displaced by a soldier, penniless, and on the run from the law. Still, a woman Clancy once loved was happy – a rare situation. Clancy envied Washington. What did Clancy have to do to achieve Washington's bliss and financial security? Start a world war?

In the verdigris green dining room, while Martha sat waiting for her husband to finish bawling out a slave for breaking something worth less than a shilling, Clancy took the opportunity to kneel and take Martha's hand.

"I was so sorry to hear of Patsy's passing. What a dear girl."

Clancy met Patsy, Martha and Daniel Custis's daughter, when she was twelve, and had taken her out to the stables and given her her first kiss. Clancy promised to come for her when she came of age – he regretted they weren't living in Scotland, where she would be of age and he could have run off with her on the spot – but three weeks later he encountered Sarah, and that was the death of yet another promise.

Martha smiled and struggled to hold back her tears. Patsy had died after one of her seizures; she was only seventeen. Mr. Clancy was so charming, Martha hoped he'd stay for a few months. The way he looked at her, she was certain she could convince him to have a word with her husband about keeping his damned dogs out of the house.

The colonel's barking ceased, and Clancy quickly kissed Martha's hand and stood as Washington entered the dining room.

Clancy and Washington sat, and a slave placed a roasted chicken before Washington. Washington picked up the carving knife and fork.

"Oh, please, let me!" said Clancy. "As long as I'm showing off the few skills I still possess."

Washington handed Clancy the carving knife and fork. Clancy leapt to his feet and in the blink of an eye carved a paper-thin slice of chicken, put it on a plate and handed it to Martha. Washington admired the thin slice. But when he looked up and saw Clancy with knife in hand –

"My God...now I remember where I first saw you," said Washington.

Clancy dropped the knife.

"The French and Indian War," said Washington. "Monongahela."

Clancy sat down, grimacing.

"I cannot tell a lie..." Clancy said, "because I cannot think of one."

"In which regiment did you serve?"

"I wasn't exactly *in* a regiment...but I did attack one. I was with the Shawnee."

Martha gasped. The slaves glanced at one another and quickly slipped out of the room and out of the line of fire.

"You were a mercenary," said Washington.

"No, a devoted son. 'Twas my mother's tribe. I am half savage." Clancy hated that word, but he thought he'd better speak in the colonel's terms in the colonel's house. Clancy also refrained from pointing out that the British had wronged the Indians and broken countless treaties, and that Clancy had, in fact, attacked British regiments twice, *nyah nyah!* But Clancy knew if he said the words, "Fort Necessity," Washington, still stinging from that humiliating surrender, would reach for that carving knife, and Clancy would be forced to make Mrs. Washington a widow. At Monongahela, the colonel had two horses shot out from under him and his coat was pierced by four musket balls; he survived the French and Indian War without a scratch and his reputation intact. Clearly, the Almighty, or Allah, or the Fates intended him to do something. Getting stabbed in the neck with a fork by The Bastard of Redbeard and dying atop a roasted chicken was probably not it. Clancy kept his mouth shut.

"What is your Indian name, sir?" Washington asked.

Clancy slid down in his chair and muttered some vowels and consonants that bounced off the Washingtons' ears. They waited for Clancy to translate into their mother tongue.

"*Chocolate Nose.*"

Mrs. Washington tried to maintain her indignation and not laugh. Washington looked at Clancy, then called, "WILLIAM!"

William Lee ran in. "Colonel?"

"No Madeira – bring out the chocolate."

"Yes, Colonel," and Mr. Lee ran out.

Mrs. Washington burst into laughter. Washington picked up the carving knife.

"Well…" shrugged Washington, "We can't choose our mother, can we? God knows I didn't…" Washington carved a chunk of chicken. "And what is your father's name?"

"Redbeard!"

In unison, the Washingtons dropped their cutlery.

William Lee marched Clancy down the hill away from the mansion, past the rifle-toting overseer.

Washington had heard the rumors for years, but thought Clancy was just posing as Redbeard's son to get attention. Clancy bore no resemblance to Roderick Redbeard. They had to be half-brothers – like Washington and Lawrence. But considering how close Washington and Lawrence had been, "half-brother" was a technicality. It was hard to believe Clancy and Roderick were even related, let alone spurted out of the same penis.

Washington wondered if Roderick hired Clancy to spy on him, to find out if Washington was enlarging his house, if his wife was wearing the latest fashions, and if he had at least one room painted verdigris green. Washington was glad he bought the armonica (on credit, as was almost everything in the mansion). It showed he was wealthy enough to buy frivolities. Roderick Redbeard would think twice about selling *him* third-rate merchandise again.

Should Washington accidentally shoot Clancy in the back as he was marched away? Would anyone miss him? Would the

Freemasons kick him out for killing a brother? Washington was still quick of temper, but now slow to pull the trigger, remembering his hot-headed days in the French and Indian War, when it cost him dearly (not to mention the lives of the men around him). Why, people around the globe blamed *him* for starting that world war! Just because he was a redhead!! He wished he could cannon the lot of them!!!

Washington's brother Lawrence had told young George spellbinding stories of attending Appleby Grammar School in England with a spawn of Redbeard, a redhead five years his junior, but his superior in intellect. Washington did arithmetic and realized "Fancy Pants Redbeard" was indeed Clancy. *So that's why those breeches Clancy wore at dinner looked familiar…* And Lawrence had once sailed with Father Redbeard himself to Jamaica during the War of Jenkins' Ear, long after the former pirate had handed his own shipmates over to the authorities. When young George asked for a bedtime story about the famed pirate, Lawrence delivered a most disappointing description: "A drunken idiot, card cheat, serial rapist and a jerk – but he had a nice smile."

It amazed Washington that Clancy was so affable and chivalrous. Bitter roots sometimes yield sweet fruit. Washington now regretted throwing Clancy out of his house. But…Clancy was a Redbeard. And Washington remembered the rumors that The Glass Musician of Williamsburg had killed seven men at the Battle of Culloden with a teaspoon. Washington made a mental note to count the silverware, and hoped William would shake down Clancy before pushing him into the Potomac. Washington was on the verge of going down the hill and shaking down Clancy himself – these slaves, they never took the initiative! – when Washington's wife called:

"Old Man! I am a little hungry."

Washington thought skipping a few meals would help Mrs. Washington fit into her old gowns and save the family from impending bankruptcy from constantly purchasing larger and larger gowns, but, unlike Clancy, Washington was a cautious man. He hoped his caution would be rewarded, one day.

"Coming, Old Woman."

As they approached thick vegetation, where he presumed Washington's men were waiting to cut his throat, Clancy pondered, "Scalping a regiment, forgivable, having a pirate for a father, apparently, not. What shipment did my father plunder from Colonel Washington?" Clancy knew Washington held grudges; if he felt slighted, you were on his shit list – forever.

"It's not your father my master hates. It's your brother Roderick," said Mr. Lee. "He sold my master some slaves that ran off the day after he bought them. Word around the slave quarters is Roderick's brother interfered."

"I only gave them horses and led them to the frontier! The colonel needs to do some of his own chores around the farm – he's getting paunchy."

Mr. Lee said, "By the way, thanks for the chocolate and pie the other evening."

"My pleasure."

Mr. Lee took Clancy behind the thick vegetation, out of view from the mansion and the overseer. There were no men waiting for Clancy, just a saddled copper horse.

Mr. Lee asked Clancy, eyebrow raised, "*You* scalped white men?"

What was so hard to believe about that? Clancy thought. He nodded.

Mr. Lee reached out, and shook Clancy's hand, Masonically. Clancy grinned. He had heard that good black men, led by Prince Hall in New England, were working on becoming better men.

"I'd say *God bless you, Clancy Redbeard*, but I doubt the odds of Him ever doing that. You're going to be traveling east, Brother Clancy."

"Brother Mr. Lee, I must go south. My wife is sleeping with a philistine."

"Go east," said Mr. Lee. "A rider is delivering these to every house between Savannah and Boston–"

Mr. Lee unfolded a broadside: *REWARD for the Capture of*

THE BASTARD OF REDBEARD, by the CHURCH for ROBBERY and ASSAULT...

"Well, it would be good to see my daughter," said Clancy. "Her mother, on the other hand…"

Mr. Lee handed the reins of the saddled horse to Clancy. "Clancy Redbeard is such a bad man. The son of a pirate robs a poor, poor church. Oh, and look, he stole a horse."

Clancy mounted the horse. "Are we squared? Is a serving of pie and chocolate equal to a horse?"

"It was really good chocolate."

Thus, though Mr. Lee was enslaved and technically not a Freemason, he and Clancy met upon the level, and parted upon the square.

XI
IN SCOTLAND WITH BENJAMIN FRANKLIN AND DAVID HUME

Clancy loathed tobacco. It destroyed precious soil, was so difficult to grow, men resorted to enslaving others to work their fields, and the finished product was addictive, stank, and stained one's teeth. But as his worsening luck would have it, the first ship he found crossing the Atlantic was a tobacco transport to Glasgow. Clancy contemplated scuttling the ship, but realized he'd simply create the demand for more enslaved labor to replace the lost tobacco. Clancy spent most of the month-long voyage standing at the ship's bow, enjoying the sea air and trying not to think.

After making sure his Scottish daughter and second wife, Fiona, were being treated well by the new drunken husband, Clancy would borrow a musical instrument and earn enough to send for Sarah and the twins. Gowan No Last Name, the

Baptist Preacher, would help with the arrangements. To Sarah, Glasgow would seem like Williamsburg without the lethal summers. Virginia was flooded with Scots fleeing war and poverty – situations in which Clancy flourished. Clancy was not most men. His ancestors were Highlanders: their blood was the fighting, not immigrating type, except for Father Redbeard, who came to America sometime before 1700. What his first name was or to which clan he once belonged was a mystery. Clancy thrice overheard the story about Father's best drinking friend who, one night in a fit of rage, shouted "Campbell!" at Father, and the next day, the friend was found in an alley, throat slit. Whether the friend was calling Father by his proper name, or his enemies', or if their fight was even about the Massacre of Glencoe, Clancy could never determine. *Redbeard* was certainly an emulation of *Blackbeard*. Father stole everything; why would his name be an exception? What Clancy did know was that his paternal ancestors had all been killed when Father, a young man of twenty-three, went to the English, volunteered the location of his family's hiding place in exchange for a commission, happily helped the English slaughter them all, and sailed to the New World to kill Indians, which included most of Clancy's maternal ancestors.

After Father sent Clancy away to Appleby Grammar School, Clancy spent holidays in Glasgow with his Irish auntie, Anne Bonny, Father's "sister." Clancy never asked what Aunt Anne's true relationship to him was, knowing any answer would most likely be a lie. Clancy presumed Aunt Anne was one of Father's acquisitions, perhaps won in a card game and kept as housekeeper and nanny for Clancy.

Over the years, Clancy's face lost his Indian mother's stoicism and seemed more and more white, until no one ever asked him, "Where are you from?" or, as he heard frequently as a child, "What *are* you?" His mother never looked Clancy in the eye, and now he could barely remember what she looked like. As Clancy departed on the ship to England to attend Appleby, Father set fire to all Clancy's drawings of his mother and tossed them into the sea, like a paper Viking funeral.

Clancy presumed Mother disliked him because he reminded her of Father…perhaps Clancy was the one who was won in a card game and given to Mother in exchange for some wrong done to her or her tribe. But then why did Clancy so resemble Father? True, owners often grew to look like their pets, but Father spent more time with his capuchin monkey than with Clancy. Or was "Mother" won in a card game…?

Anne Bonny and Calico Jack were rumored to have had a child in Cuba. Was he that child? Clancy had a friend at Appleby whose "sister," twelve years his senior, was, in fact, his mother. Aunt Anne was about twenty-three years older than Clancy… Like Aunt Anne, Mary Read escaped hanging by claiming she was pregnant. Was Mary Read his real mother? Trying to piece the puzzle together made Clancy's head hurt.

After Redbeard died, Clancy asked people who knew Father what they really thought of him. They said nothing, but their actions spoke volumes. No one wanted Clancy to come live with them, meet their daughters, loan him money, do business with him, or even sit at the same table. Everyone remembered his father's multiple betrayals and assumed the rotten apple didn't fall far from the pirate. The only people eager to make Clancy's acquaintance were criminals, and only because they assumed he would buy them whisky and introduce them to the lowest of whores. Clancy preferred fine wines and finer women, and his new friends either left him in the dust when he refused to join their illegal activities, or worse, tried to pin their crimes on him.

Now, save for Roderick, Clancy's siblings were all dead and their wives and friends refused to talk, and Aunt Anne was mad as a hatter, so Clancy would never know the truth. What he did know was enough: that no one wanted him. Considering his family's tradition of exterminating relations who did not toe the line, Clancy felt grateful just to be alive, to live another day for the chance to achieve what all Scots most long for: a good death in battle. In his youth, he had made quite an effort to achieve that.

At Culloden, Clancy was twenty-three years old, the same

age that Father betrayed his family to the English. At last, it was Clancy's chance for redemption. Clancy joined the *Royal Écossais*, a Scottish regiment in the French army. It seemed the most professional of all the motley forces assembled under Bonnie Prince Charlie, but Clancy soon discovered most of his fellow "soldiers" were press-ganged into it. At the battle, Clancy killed seven English, two certainly limped forever after, and two he mortally wounded, but he had to flee grapeshot before he could put the men out of their misery. Twenty-eight years on, rarely a day went by when Clancy didn't think of those eleven men. He wished he could find the survivors, widows and orphans, make sure they were managing all right, apologize, and see if they needed help around the house.

After the battle was lost, Clancy went to Fiona's father's tavern, drank for three days and, according to ten witnesses, proposed to Fiona, who was, at the time, five years old. Clancy had just seen more than a thousand men slaughtered around him; anything could have come out of his mouth. Fiona promised to marry him when she came of age. Alas, they kept their promise, though Fiona had a considerable wait. After making his drunken promise, Clancy went to London and married his beloved first wife, who died nine months later. Clancy then sailed around the world three times, searching for the perfect woman. He finally gave up and returned to London and his favorite brothel, where he met Jane. The brothel was low on candles the night she and Clancy copulated. Jane only felt his size and knew he'd give her a big, healthy son who would be handy around the brothel. Imagine her horror when, in the morning, Jane realized she'd let herself be impregnated by a redhead. Clancy insisted he gave Jane ample warning by stating his surname – twice – but Jane was not the brightest woman in the world. She did indeed have a big, healthy son, Patrick. Clancy supported them but refused to marry Jane; this was during the years when Clancy topped Roderick's hit list, and Clancy wanted no wife nor heir in the path of his brother's wrath.

Fiona finally caught Clancy when he was rebounding from

missing his chance to marry Martha Dandridge Custis. Fiona was by that time an elderly eighteen-year-old, not twelve, the age she could have legally wed Clancy. Nine months later they had a daughter, Margaret. Less than a month after that, Fiona exchanged Clancy, who spent half the night in the tavern drinking, for another drunken husband who drank at home and fell asleep in his chair after only one whisky. Clancy didn't blame her. The new husband was a better bargain and easier to clean up after. More importantly, he was on the winning side at Culloden and had a pension, so Fiona and Clancy's daughter would never starve.

With all his Glasgow drinking friends now dead, and no Aunt Anne living there, Clancy had no desire to go to Scotland. Still, it was the right thing, to check up on his daughter, see if she needed anything, tell her she was loved, even if it was just by him. And then he had to get Sarah and the twins away from that uncultured iron-burned redcoat, and far from Roderick.

As he disembarked in Glasgow, Clancy put one of his last coins in a busking bagpiper's tin cup, impressed that the piper played the piobaireachd *MacDougall's Gathering*, not some cheesy tune like *Cock o' the North*, and that the piper was thumbing his nose at the Dress Act of 1746, decked out head-to-toe in Highland garb.

"Goin' fer a nice rest in jail?" Clancy grinned when the piper finished.

The piper grinned as he swabbed his bass drone. "Och, done tha'; goin' fer my second offense, when I'll be *transported to any of His Majesty's plantations beyond the seas, there to remain for the space of seven years*."

"I don't think it's going to be much of a holiday."

"Anythin' tae get off this fockin' island. Ye call this summer?" the piper growled as freezing rain pelted their faces.

As Clancy walked to the east end of the city, an old farmer chewing tobacco squinted at him.

"Redbeard?"

"Aye!"

The farmer spat on Clancy's shoe. He made a big show of turning his back on Clancy, which afforded Clancy the opportunity to snatch the farmer's money bag.

"Nice to be hame," Clancy said as he watched the now-penniless farmer go down the hill. The tobacco-laced spittle was easily wiped off and worked like a polish. Clancy wished he'd hit both shoes so he could be symmetrical.

Clancy wanted to buy a new suit, but knew he should put his family first. Look what happened in Williamsburg when he went to the tailor instead of straight home. He'd buy his wife and daughter gifts, smooth things over, and then get the new suit. Clancy went to market, and bought a big bouquet, and spent two entire minutes studying a shelf of dolls. They all looked equally useless to him. Why did women get angry when you gave them useful gifts like a Franklin Stove so they would not die of blood poisoning from burns, or a new broom to make sweeping more efficient? But he would let his girls have the soon-to-be-dead flowers and the little fake human. Clancy pointed to the biggest doll and handed one of the farmer's coins to the woman minding the stand.

"Can you tell me where I might find One-Whisky's wife, the former Fiona Redbeard?" Clancy asked.

"I can."

Clancy waited.

"*Will* you please tell me where she is?"

"I will."

But she didn't.

"Then, please do so," Clancy replied, his smile weakening.

"In the hill."

"What, in a Picts house?" Fiona would rather die than live in that kind of dug-out house, no matter how warm, thrifty, and practical. Clancy rephrased his query one last time, preparing to bash the doll over the woman's head: "Where does Fiona live?"

"In the hill!"

The woman pointed to the nearby hill, where no one lived.

Clancy stood on the hill, holding the flowers and the doll. He knelt and put the flowers against the Celtic cross inscribed *Fiona Redbeard, died 1770, Age 29.* Clancy leaned the doll against the smaller Celtic cross, *Margaret Redbeard, died 1770, Age 10.* The new drunken husband had not drunk the water from the well and remarried a week after their funeral. In death, he had given them back to Clancy: he did not want Fiona and Margaret sullying his family's name for eternity.

Clancy took the little figure of Jesus from his pocket and leaned it against Fiona's cross. He dug a hole next to his daughter's grave, placed the doll in, and smoothed the doll's petticoat with his elbow, carefully, so as not to get dirt on it. He. He started to gently cover the hole with earth, but then grabbed fistfuls of soil and bashed them down over the doll. He didn't care he was getting his cuffs dirty.

Clancy sat on the hill for the rest of the afternoon. Dark clouds formed. Church bells tolled. Clancy stared into space, trying not to think.

And then he saw a kite flying against the dark clouds.

Clancy ran to see who held the kite. Lightning flashed. He saw the silk kite had a sharp wire protruding from the top. His eyes followed the wet string down to a key tied to the string, and to the sixty-eight-year-old man holding the string. Clancy could not believe his eyes.

"DOCTOR FRANKLIN, DOCTOR FRANKLIN! I've read every edition of *Poor Richard's Almanack* and all your essays and I used to drive my wife mad by spending our money on importing *The Philadelphia Gazette* to Williamsburg so I could read your essays and I played your glass armonica at Colonel Washington's home at Mount Vernon and I used to install lightning rods – Franklin Rods! – on the steeples of churches until I realized I was protecting criminal organizations from the wrath of God!"

Franklin was thrilled. His sixty-three-year-old companion, David Hume, was annoyed. This was *his* native land. *He* should have been the one to be recognized.

"A Franklin Fanatic," sneered Hume. "Soon, they'll be putting your portrait on dinner plates."

"And chamber pots," said Franklin.

Clancy caught his breath: "And your Franklin stove, I made some modifications so it doesn't smoke as much, I hope you don't mind, and your catheter – much appreciated after I fell off my horse, broke my leg and couldn't get out of bed for a month."

"Another useless invention," poo-pooed Hume.

Clancy grabbed Hume's cravat and pulled him until they were nose-to-nose.

"Useless? Wait a couple of years, Mr. Hume, and enjoy pissing all over yourself when you're on your deathbed, you toffee-nosed Edinburgh philosophizing git. Until you make the leap into the marital contract, stop killing trees and other men's time by writing essays on love and marriage, virginal know-it-all. You exchange a few letters with Hippolyte de Saujon, and you think you're Don Juan. No wonder you're so against polygamy – you can't even get one date!"

"You did recognize me!" gasped Hume. Clancy made Hume's day!

Franklin almost lost his grip on the kite string, suddenly realizing who Clancy's father was. Franklin had been so absorbed in being flattered, it blinded him. (He constantly broke every rule of conduct he invented for others. Franklin was amazed no one ever called him out on it. *Ah, the advantages of being old, charming and witty…and rich.*) Franklin had also been thrown by the young man's smile: it was warm and genuine, not flashed solely to disarm you before he stole your purse. You only saw the resemblance when Clancy was angry.

"Redbeard!"

A flash of lightning and huge clap of thunder sealed the proclamation.

"The heavens do not approve of you, Mr. Redbeard," said Hume.

Franklin pointed to the skies. "You think this is the opinion of God? Mr. Hume, you appear not to have read my writings – my Copley Medal-winning writings–"

"*On Account of His Curious Experiments and Observations on Electricity,*" Clancy chirped.

Franklin smiled at Clancy. *He knows my work, not just my name! I like THIS son of Redbeard.* Clancy had written over two hundred letters to Dr. Franklin, but most had been intercepted by a jealous English clerk, or by Franklin's wife (*My husband roving with The Bastard of Redbeard, just what I need* thought Deborah Franklin).

"Curiosity killed the cat," said Hume.

"Indeed?" said Franklin. "Put your knuckle to the key, Mr. Hume."

"No, thank you, 'Doctor' Franklin," Hume scoffed at Franklin's honorific, and inwardly lamented he would never receive one. Universities – seminaries in secular disguise – spurned anyone rumored to be skeptical of the Almighty's existence, or worse, was skeptical of The Church's authority. Universities were also leery of lifelong bachelors. Dr. Franklin, on the other hand, was longtime married, had a longtime mistress, il and legitimate children, had lost a son (had he lost a daughter, *yawn*...), and was on the verge of being widowed. He had stuck his fingers into so many of life's pies, and yet had all his limbs, was rich, and universally admired – how could you not reward such a man?

Franklin held out the key to Hume. "Oh, come now, Mr. Hume, what are you afraid of?"

Clancy had enough. "Oh, for Christ's sake–"

Clancy put his knuckle to the key, just as lightning struck the kite. A strong charge hit Clancy's knuckle and sent him tumbling down the hill, knocking him out cold.

David Hume, in a fancy red frock coat and powdered wig, looking directly at the viewer, dark background

roggy Clancy opened his eyes, and saw Franklin and Hume sitting across from him, drinking ale. Clancy looked at the clientele and realized they were in The Cat and Bagpipes, an overpriced tavern with terrible food. Why did he have to be so dramatic and get himself knocked out? He could have warned Dr. Franklin about this tourist trap. Clancy looked down at the table. A drunken hand had carved *James Boswell and Doctor Johnson Ate Here 1773*. Poor Corsica Boswell was still drifting after being rejected as a Naider Raider: Rafe said he had far too many Edinburgh lawyers, and needed more Glaswegians to ballast *JUSTICE* (that, and there was no way he was letting that anti-abolitionist drunk within mile of his daughter).

"You're writing your autobiography?" sniffed Hume.

He wasn't, but Clancy wondered why he hadn't thought to write about his adventures. He wanted to live, and not spend the rest of his days in court, that's why. Perhaps in two hundred fifty years, some brilliant and insightful woman, who would make a fortune writing and publishing the finest biography of Rafe Naider, as well as her own brilliant memoirs documenting her amazing and heroic adventures, would go on to write *his* life story...then Clancy realized Hume was addressing Dr. Franklin.

"I am simply living up to the English's expectations of all colonists," Franklin said, tired of constantly soothing Hume's glasslike pride. He wished his usual traveling companion, John Pringle, was here instead of Huffy Hume.

"Well, you're no Galileo or Newton," said Hume.

Clancy reached across the table to grab Hume's cravat, when Franklin held up a finger and mouthed, *one*. Franklin held up his next finger, *two*, and then his next finger, *three*. Hume's eyes closed, his chin hit his chest, and he began snoring.

"My latest discovery," Franklin smiled. "If you cease fighting with a Scotsman for three seconds, he shuts down."

"My mother's blood must give me immunity," Clancy mused. "If only your technique worked on members of Parliament. Remaining silent encourages them to attack. Just look at the American colonies. We relax for one minute; they levy another unjust tax on us."

"Parliament will do right. The Crown is reasonable—"

"Ha!" laughed the serving woman who banged another ale in front of Franklin. Unlike Franklin, she knew that of which she spoke; she had worked in almost all the British colonies. Clancy winked at her. He hoped he could stay conscious long enough to ask her to go to bed with him.

Clancy said to Franklin, "You must join Rafe Naider!"

"Naider must temper his rhetoric. He's always too impatient."

"All the laws he helped create in the sixties are being torn to shreds. All the unjust acts levied by Parliament that he helped quash, they're returning. We need you, at home: our King of America."

"Careful, young Redbeard. That is bordering on treason."

"Then, America's Father."

Franklin liked that. He had helped found The Union Fire Company, The Pennsylvania Hospital for the Sick-Poor and Insane, The American Philosophical Society, The Library Company... He began to think about free public education.

"Thank you for your letters, Mr. Redbeard. I apologize for replying to only one of them."

"*Clancy*. You're a busy man, Dr. Franklin. I appreciated you taking the time to write me."

"Did you take my advice?"

"About taking an older mistress? Oh, Dr. Franklin...*wise men don't need advice, fools won't take it*. Incidentally, how long has it been since you've seen your wife?"

"Er, uh–" (Almost ten years, but only Mrs. Franklin and her family and friends were counting.)

"Dr. Franklin, when I was angry, you saw who I was. In your travels, I presume you ran into my father?"

"He ran into an early prototype of my armonica. Kicked it over at a party, to be precise."

Clancy winced. "I know it's a semitransparent instrument, but how drunk was he?"

"Well, before he smashed the glass bowls and ground them into the carpet with his boot, he screamed, *stop that thing, it's driving me mad!* So, I always presumed it was purposely done."

Clancy's jaw dropped. His dream meeting with Dr. Franklin was turning into a nightmare. Franklin said, "You didn't know? I was sure he'd told you the tale."

"My God, no!" But Clancy knew that if there was anyone on the planet who would purposely smash an armonica, it was Father. "How much do I – they cost–" Clancy reached into his nearly empty pockets. "I'm sorry, Dr. Franklin. I'll pay you back, even it takes me–"

"No need, my young friend. When you meet another honest man in similar distress, you must pay me by giving the sum to him."

Clancy hanged his head and burst into tears. The doctor poured Clancy another whisky.

The next morning, Clancy and Franklin left Hume, still face down on the Cat and Bagpipes table, and went for a long walk in the grassy hills. They were miles from town, when Clancy stepped on something that made a loud *crunch*. He looked down.

"Good God–"

A human skeleton lay in the grass. Clancy examined the remains. Apart from the humerus Clancy broke, there were no signs of skeletal trauma. The poor wretch still wore his leather boots; his wool clothing was in rags, picked apart by birds for their nests. There was a fishing pole by his side. He had been heading for the sea.

"Famine," diagnosed Dr. Franklin.

"I fear the same thing will happen in America," said Clancy. "The divide between the rich and poor is widening, creating a ditch into which many will fall. We must break free from the grip of this empire."

"No, no, we must be friends with the mother country." Dr. Franklin loved living in London, far from his wife in Philadelphia, and was perceived by the English as a diplomat, soothing relations with those barbaric colonists – until the Hutchinson Letters incident. Now everyone in London thought Franklin, that prime conductor of agitation, was hiding in his house in the appropriately named Craven Street. Even George III asked Lord Dartmouth, Secretary of State for the Colonies, "Where is Dr. Franklin?" It had been a miserable year, and Franklin wanted back in the game. "You must not stir things up, young man."

Clancy said, "Is that why you wrote the essay, *Rules by Which a Great Empire May be Reduced to a Small One*? And that *Edict by the King of Prussia* – what kind of peace-making is that, Doctor? What game are you playing? You want America's great forests to go the way of Scotland's?" Clancy pointed to the treeless hills. "To the bottom of the oceans? *Rule Britannia!* Until she runs out of lumber for her ships. *Colonialism*? It's colonial exploitation. Using up other nation's resources, how bloody rude. Do you want New England to become New Ireland?"

Rather than debate him, Franklin decided it best to let the young Redbeard get things out of his system, and then take him back to The Cat and Bagpipes, where he could resume drinking and fighting with Dr. – er, Mr. Hume.

Clancy looked down at the sea. His legs wobbled – a hangover from the lightning bolt, but which Franklin mistook for sea legs.

"You have a hankering for the sea! I tried to stow away when I was fifteen, as did my son. He's a bastard, too…but now, the Royal Governor of New Jersey!"

Clancy snorted.

Franklin noted, "Like your father, he became legitimate."

"But your son did not send his shipmates to the gallows to save his own neck."

"Well, not yet…you must not be so hard on your father. Had he not done what he did, you, young man, would not exist."

"And the world would be better for it."

Franklin put his arm around Clancy. "You must find an outlet for your talents, as I did."

Clancy whispered, "You're William Death…aren't you?"

Franklin took a long, deep breath and smiled.

Clancy said, "Raider Kelvin said that's exactly how you would respond. *Richard Saunders, Alice Addertongue, Anthony Afterwit, Silence Dogood…*" Clancy listed just a few of Franklin's pen names. "*William Death – Captain Death*. It's you. It's *you*."

"Clancy, Clancy…*Clancy*, wonderful name. It means *red warrior*."

"It does?"

"You know what you are, Clancy?" Franklin dug into his waistcoat pocket. "Someone gave me this souvenir from the French and Indian War…."

Franklin unfolded an aging piece of paper and proudly showed Clancy his famous *Join or Die* cartoon: a snake cut into eight pieces.

"This is you: the noble rattlesnake in pieces. But when you pull yourself together and strike, the world will never be the same. I've heard how well you fought at Culloden."

"We lost."

"If every Scot was a Clancy, every Englishman would be speaking Gaelic."

Clancy felt like crying. Franklin sighed, "There is only one way out of your current paralysis, young Captain Redbeard…"

Dr. Franklin pulled Clancy closer, and whispered:

"Kill your brother."

Clancy thought he must have misheard. "What?"

Franklin said, "I, too, had an older bullying brother. I used those pen names to get my articles past James – he tore up everything *Benjamin Franklin* wrote. But my brother was not a threat to civilization. If you are sincere about protecting America, kill Roderick."

Clancy turned and ran for his life, down the hill and towards the sea.

Franklin sighed, pulled a flask from his coat, and took a drink – and not of chocolate.

XII
TO PHILADELPHIA WITH
THOMAS PAIN(e)

I n the Glasgow gazettes, a cryptic notice from Gowan No Last Name, the Baptist preacher, warned Clancy that church authorities in the colonies were greeting every ship from Glasgow with warrants and pistols. Clancy went south and boarded the *LONDON PACKET*. He had just enough for the fare back to America, thanks to David Hume's purse, to which he had helped himself at The Cat and Bagpipes (Clancy felt justified; Hume once told Clancy he was drinking watered-down whisky – it wasn't – and then challenged Clancy to a card game). Clancy dropped Hume's gold watch and coins onto the steward's table, and went aboard, taking his passenger position, at the ship's bow. If he couldn't be the captain or man the helm, this was the third best position. Well, perhaps the fourth. He had fallen out of one too many fighting tops to risk it at his age, and his luck appeared to be running out. The other passengers were all below deck. Why were they were missing this glorious sunny day, Clancy wondered. What gloom could possibly erase this perfect afternoon?

Remembering what a failure his trip was, for starters; finding his Scottish wife and daughter were long dead – how had he not sensed it? – and being a disappointment to his third biggest hero. It was worse that Dr. Franklin had been so kind. Clancy wished the doctor had kicked him in the backside, slapped him across the face, shocked him with his turkey cooker – something, anything to jolt Clancy out of his usual ways. That bolt of lightning hadn't done the trick.

Clancy pulled a bottle of whisky from his pocket, and realized his meager supply and whatever liquor was on board wouldn't be enough to get him through the upcoming eight-week voyage. Clancy was near tears, when he heard someone else crying. He looked over and saw another soul in even more pain than he. Clancy put his whisky back in his pocket, and forgot all about it, for he had something to do: *Cheer up that man!* With his kindly manner and sewing skills, Clancy should have been a doctor. He had sincerely tried to become one, studying medical books in his youth, but Father Redbeard had the lowest opinion of doctors: "All quacks," said he, and he used Clancy's books as firewood. When Clancy pointed out that he could tend his father's crews, Father said idiots who got themselves shot or couldn't handle pain deserved to die; besides, it meant fewer crew to divvy up the booty. After Father died, no doctor would take Clancy as an apprentice: an offspring of Redbeard entrusted with sharp instruments and laudanum?

The crying man was in his mid-thirties, wearing a wind-blown wig, and clothes as ragged as Clancy's. He felt a strong, warm arm around his shoulders. He looked up and saw Clancy's smiling face.

"We are going on an adventure to the New World!"

"Yet another chance to fail," moaned the crying man.

"Yes," admitted Clancy, "that probably is the most truthful way of seeing the situation…but fantasy and self-delusion makes one's destiny so much more palatable! You leave behind many women?"

The man howled. "My first wife, died in childbirth…"

"As did mine."

"…my second wife…I married my landlord's daughter."

Clancy had almost fallen into that trap. "The things we men do to pay the rent."

"I have failed at every profession. Corset maker…"

"'Tis a sin to bind women," Clancy declared. "And whose bright idea was it to make women resemble upside down bagpipe chanters? Why is a conical shape preferable to an hourglass, or a cello? But you were saying?"

"I also failed as a teacher, a preacher…"

"If your students and flocks failed to take your advice, 'twas their loss."

"…tax clerk–"

"I rejoice you failed at that."

"I spent so much time petitioning Parliament for higher salaries for my fellow excisemen, my tobacco shop failed…."

"Good for you, sir – nasty stuff. Tobacco and taxes on the poor, that is; fighting abuse and tyranny, most honorable."

"…as a boy, I tried to join Captain Death's crew. My father caught me and hauled me off his ship…."

"Captain Death…" Clancy sighed.

"…Rafe Naider wouldn't take me aboard the *JUSTICE*…."

"You and I, we really are on the same boat."

"…and I failed as a privateer."

"Next time, skip the governmental middlemen and go straight into piracy."

The man pulled a letter from his torn coat. "All my possessions, sold to avoid debtor's prison. I have only this letter of introduction. It might as well be the order for my execution!"

The man dropped the unsealed letter on the deck and sobbed. Clancy picked up the letter. "From Dr. Franklin!" he exclaimed.

"The 'Good Doctor' has doomed me to a life of misery and poverty, without the company of women."

Clancy read the letter. "...*his most excellent mind is best suited for that of an...author.*"

The man howled at the thought.

"Dr. Franklin's sense of humor grows warped as he ages," Clancy said, wondering what this gentle man did to make Benjamin Franklin so vengeful. "No matter. We'll be friends, Mister—"

Clancy looked at the name on Dr. Franklin's letter.

"—Pain." The poor man couldn't get a break.

"Clancy Redbeard," Clancy smiled. "*Clancy.*"

"Thomas," said Pain.

"*Tom,*" winked Clancy, putting his arm around Tom. A new friend and fresh sea air! The two men stood at the bow together, focused on the horizon as the ship went out to sea. Then Tom spoke the words which most of mankind dreaded above all others:

"Will you read my manuscript?"

L uckily for Tom, Clancy wasn't most of mankind. Clancy enjoyed reading rough drafts and discovering new authors. He had met Jonathan Swift and Daniel Defoe in his youth, and derived much pleasure from knowing it was his encouragement and modest patronage that kept many authors from chucking themselves off bridges, or worse, taking actual jobs. How Clancy wished he had a printing press. Perhaps that was his calling? In the cabin Clancy and Tom shared, next to three other seasick and feverish cabin passengers, with the stench of one hundred twenty indentured passengers in the hold, Clancy worked his way through the two-thousand-page manuscript. Tom huddled in his berth, sweating and pale, though in better spirits now that someone showed interest in his writings.

On page four hundred twenty-one, Clancy laughed.

Puzzled, Tom said, "It's funny?"

Clancy replied, "It's just...common sense!"

*L*ONDON PACKET tossed in the waves. When the last two able-bodied sailors doubled over with stomach pains, Clancy ordered them below and took the helm. He was alone at the stern, except for an old, bearded man wrapped in an oilcloth sitting by the railing. The drinking water had sickened the passengers and crew. Clancy feared well water and always waited for rain. He would lean back, open his mouth, and milk the rain from his long hair.

Clancy called to the old man in the oilcloth, "Sir, are you all right?"

The old man nodded, his face downcast. Clancy had seen him comforting and holding the hands of ill passengers in the hold. Clancy wanted to become the friend of such a caring person, but when Clancy had approached him, the old man turned away. Clancy felt as though he was forever walking a tightrope, always being either too standoffish, or obnoxiously pushy. How he wished he had The Franklin Touch. He would have to do something. People admired Dr. Franklin for inventing something that might one day save their lives, and they approached him with deference, which in turn made Franklin relaxed and inviting...whereas Clancy always wondered if people walking towards him were about to stab him for some wrong Father Redbeard did them, and though he always tried to be friendly, he often unconsciously put his hand on the grip of his sword, or in his coat, as though reaching for a pistol, and didn't realize what he'd done until the person had quickly walked away. No, he would have to do something....

Sickly Tom, a blanket over his head and holding a cup of

chocolate, came from below deck. What he saw made him stop in his tracks. At the helm, Clancy was in his element. Clancy did not look the fool. He was Captain Redbeard.

Lightning flashed.

"Tom! Back to bed!"

"My manuscript! Where is it?"

"Keeping me warm–" Clancy opened his great coat, showing the pages poking out from his waistcoat.

Tom wailed. "It's only good for lining coats and starting fires...and you laughed all the way through it."

"In delight, Tom! You have a great mind. And I hope you don't mind...I added an *E* to the end of your family name, to increase sales. Softens it just enough to stop frightening people."

"But there's already a Thomas Paine – the privateer."

"Privateer, my ass!" Clancy spat to the side. "When he got too old to plunder, he laundered Captain Kidd's goodies. Claimed he sailed with Henry Morgan. And I'm really George the Second's oldest son! Become a famous author, Tom, and everyone will forget that other Paine."

Tom spat into the wind, and the spit flew right back into his eye.

Tom handed Clancy the cup of chocolate. Clancy was about to drink it, when he saw the old man. Clancy handed Tom the helm. The force of the wheel almost hurled Tom overboard.

Clancy walked to the old man on the tilting deck, balancing the chocolate cup on a saucer with his fingertips. He did not spill a drop.

"Sir! Please, have the last of the chocolate..."

Keeping his head down, the old man reached for the chocolate, and Clancy saw a glimpse of the feminine gloved hand. Clancy bowed, and went back to Tom, walking backwards so as not to turn his back on the...

Tom asked the ashen-faced Clancy, "Have you seen a ghost?"

"That old man...is not."

Tom whispered, "A woman? But she has a beard!"

"You haven't traveled much, have you Tom? Best not to reveal her. I have not the money to shelter her."

"And she could be another Mary Read."

"Or, God help the world, my Aunt Anne Bonny."

Clancy and Tom smiled at the "old man." Terrified smiles. *Please, don't hurt us...*

*L*ONDON *PACKET* docked on a calm afternoon. Disembarkation took longer than usual, with so many passengers too ill to walk, or dead. Two men rolled bodies onto blankets and tossed them onto a wagon. Clancy sat on the dock cradling Tom, who was near death, sweating, shaking, and terrified at the sight of corpses lining the dock.

"Are we in Hell?"

"No, Tom – Philadelphia."

"Where is Joan of Arc now? Would that heaven might inspire some New Jersey maid to spirit up her countrymen and save her fellow sufferers from ravage and ravishment!"

Clancy nodded, wiping the sweat from Tom's brow with his torn, dirty lace cuff. "These are the times that try men's souls."

Tom smiled. What a wonderful line. He hoped he would live long enough to steal it. He'd buy Clancy a drink in thanks.

A carriage pulled up to the dock, and a man holding a leather case climbed out. Clancy called, "Doctor Kearsely!"

Tom clutched Clancy's coat. "Don't leave me, Clancy!"

"I am not worthy of your company, Tom."

Clancy tucked Tom's manuscript under Tom's arm and handed the doctor a letter.

"From Dr. Franklin."

Actually, Clancy had thrown Franklin's letter overboard, and wrote a new one, describing Tom as "an ingenious worthy young man," and asking Franklin's son-in-law to help Tom obtain temporary employment as a clerk, assistant tutor, or assistant surveyor, which would give Tom a living, but plenty of free time to write. The voyage gave Clancy plenty of time to practice forging Dr. Franklin's signature.

Doctor Kearsley and his assistants picked up the ends of Tom's blanket and carried him to the carriage. Clancy watched them drive away.

Clancy asked the dockmaster, "Has *JUSTICE* docked here?"

"*JUSTICE?*" spat the dockmaster. "Luyk uh wud permid Reef Needer in ma wooder! Da jawn spoiled errythin'! 'e killedda Corvair!"

"Needer killed a corsair?" Clancy asked, quickly tuning his ear and accent to the Philadelphian – Fluffyian – axsend. He must have misheard. Naider was incapable of killing anyone, not even a pirate.

"Da CorVAIR! Wha awr ya, Spanish? Kend ya prance yer *V*s? Id wasda mosd beyoodeeful shep! Demn Reef Needer an'is lill dree 'unner fordy-sex pehg pemfled, *Unsafe a' Any Knot!* Ye, soda shep capsize' win mekin' sherp durns…sue wad?! Id seperaded da greed capdins frum da incompudend! Ef zey dininno owda compensade er 'elms, zey deserded da die!"

He sounds just like Father (without the Ts and Hs), Clancy thought. Clancy was still rubbing the accent out of his ears when the dockmaster's young son told him that *JUSTICE* had attempted to sail up the Delaware to Philadelphia but was driven back by a merchant who had twenty-four-pound guns. The boy's uncle had followed Naider to Cape May, and saw *JUSTICE* turn north. So, they were now bound for Boston after all.

Clancy hoped his voice would hold out so he could sing for his supper and a bed. Should he leave for Virginia tomorrow? Or wait for word from Gowan No Last Name to see if Sarah and the twins had left Williamsburg? Clancy stood alone on the dock, waiting for something to happen. He had been so happy on the voyage, talking to his new friend and commanding the ship, he had forgotten all about the bottle of whisky in his pocket. He needed it now —

A broadside blowing in the wind landed at his feet. He

Unsafe
at
Any Knot

The Designed-in Dangers
of Colonial American Vessels

by Rafe Naider

MAD RIVER, NEW ENGLAND
Printed by Not-Poor Richard Groffman

looked down and saw *REWARD for the Capture of* —

Could he not have one moment's rest? Clancy grabbed the broadside. He began to sway. Sea legs? He hadn't slept in two days. Clancy realized his eyes were closed. He struggled to open them. He must have fallen asleep standing up.

A canvas bag whizzed past Clancy's head and landed at his feet. It was followed by a walking stick, and what appeared to be a giant hairball. Clancy bent down and picked up the false beard.

Clancy looked up. The old man/young woman wrapped in the oil cloth stood at the ship's railing, a silhouette backlit by the sun.

"I see you've traveled some." The voice was a young man's…or an old woman's.

"You have no idea," Clancy replied. He was so tired that he didn't recognize a fellow Freemason's greeting.

"What will you do now?" the passenger asked, peeling off their gloves.

"Something," said Clancy, looking at the skyline of Philadelphia. "But what?"

"When I have free time, I always kill someone." The passenger's voice then dropped an octave. "There are so many deserving people."

The passenger dropped its feminine gloves on the dock. They were the largest women's gloves Clancy had ever seen.

"*The cat in gloves catches no mice*," said the…the…

Clancy looked up at the ship. The "old man" gracefully hopped onto the railing and flung off the oil cloth.

His long dark hair blew in the wind. He was barefoot, and wore a black shirt, black leggings, a small sword, and a dagger strapped to his thigh. He was in his early thirties, lean, and far too athletic to be a lawyer.

"We meet at last, Bastard of Redbeard!"

The man grabbed a rope, propelled himself off the railing, and landed on the dock in front of Clancy. Clancy took a step back, dropped his bottle of whisky, and fell on his ass.

The man reached down, grabbed Clancy's hand, and yanked

him off his ass. The man pulled a gold ring off his finger and slipped it on Clancy's. The ring had a skull, enclosed by a square and compasses. Above the skull was a *G.*

Before Clancy could say anything, or run for his life, he looked up and saw the man in black smiling at him in such a friendly way, Clancy did not want to pull away. They were nose-to-nose. The only time Clancy ever got that close to another man was just before giving him a Glasgow Kiss.

The man's hands were cold as ice. Clancy had always envisioned The Angel of Death as a woman in white. Clancy thought he must be dreaming, and the man would vanish if Clancy touched his face. That was how Clancy's dreams of women usually ended. He was forever reaching out to them, and just as he was about to make contact, they vanished into thin air. He had never dreamt of a man before. But it had been a long, long voyage. Clancy had not been with a woman since…when…?

As Clancy raised his hand to touch the man's ghostly white cheek, the man saw the broadside in Clancy's hand and gently took it from him.

REWARD for the Capture of –

The man unfurled the broadside.

CAPTAIN DEATH. £10,000 DEAD OR ALIVE.

The man grinned.

"In London, I was only worth five thousand!"

Captain Death wrapped himself back in the oil cloth, bent over so he was half his true height, and took Clancy's arm.

"Let's go see my ladies–"

And Death led Clancy north.

XIII
THE CHOCOLATE PIRATE

roadsides on every corner advertised *REWARD for the Capture of CAPTAIN DEATH*. Most merchants requested he be brought to them extremely dead, the most vindictive requested *Severely Disabled but Alive and Conscious*, others offered varying monetary rewards for certain body parts. Death was proud he was such a boost to the economy: bounty hunters, sheriffs, fire brigades, glassmakers, house builders, doctors, undertakers… "I cannot be caught," he told Clancy as they walked arm-in-arm up the street. "Think how many people I will put out of work."

Death took Clancy into a large house in Fairhill in North Philadelphia, where they were greeted – after the front door closed and blocked the spectacle from prying neighbors – by ten black female house slaves cheering and applauding. Death flung off his oil cloth, put his canvas bag on the floor, smiled shyly, and kissed an old woman's cheek. Death proceeded down the line, kissing the women's cheeks like a loving son, which confused Clancy to no end. When Death said, *let's go see my ladies*, Clancy thought they were going to a brothel.

Clancy tried to think: Father always called Captain Death, "My Friend," which to Father meant Drinking Friend, and the youngest a man could be to hold his liquor and keep up with Father would be…eight? Clancy was getting more confused, so he asked one of the women for a bottle of wine, uncorked it with his teeth, and drank straight from the bottle.

Delia, the cook, put her arm around a young mulatto girl, who curtsied to Death. "Bless you, for killing my sister's overseer," said Delia. "Say *thank you* to Captain Death."

"No thanks needed," said Death. "It was my honor to help." Death had a non-English accent, but Clancy couldn't identify it. It was almost lyrical. Irish? Welsh? Italian? Or that rarest of men, a sweet-natured soft-spoken Prussian?

The next woman in line handed Death a rapier: "For what you did for my family in Savannah."

"For me? Oh, my…" Death removed his old chipped small, sheathed the rapier and hugged the woman.

Delia asked, "How is your true love?"

"My 'true love' turned me in for a five-thousand-pound reward!"

The women gasped. "What did you do?" Delia asked.

Death replied, coldly, "Let's just say he will not have any future lovers."

Clancy choked on his wine.

Death looked at the décor. "So, this is John Dickinson's house."

The women nodded.

"And where is the master?" Death inquired.

The women laughed.

"Have you been freed, or does Mr. Dickinson still think he owns you?"

Delia gave a docile smile.

"I shall have a little word with him, after I finish my business in Boston…" Death patted his rapier. "Thank you, ladies! Thank you! You're all as beautiful and sweet as chocolate. Speaking of which…"

Death unsheathed the rapier, and with it ripped opened his canvas bag, spilling cocoa beans everywhere. The women screamed with delight.

Captain Death was dying.

The voyage from England had taken its toll. He had to be strong for his ladies; they had suffered through far worse than he: separated from their families, abused and starved, beaten, raped…come to think of it, their backgrounds were identical…but anyone who attacked a smaller, vulnerable person – it made Death's blood boil. His nose bled constantly, and now blood came out his ears. But he would not lie down, not yet. One more try. He needed help. His plan had been to join The Sons of Liberty, and bring with him The Bastard of Redbeard, who could captain a ship, nurse the passengers, and walk across a deck in a storm balancing a cup of chocolate on three fingers…

…but now it seemed The Bastard of Redbeard was nothing more than a useless drunk. Death watched Clancy drink glass after glass of wine. Captain Death, the terror of the seven seas, ate pie.

Clancy wore a cream silk embroidered coat. Delia had procured it for Death, but he had lost so much weight it hung off his bones, and it was far too flamboyant for his next adventure. Death asked for something very bland and dark, something Bostonians would ignore. "*You* want to be ignored?" Delia asked. Death said he would be engaging in street fights and needed something that didn't show blood. Delia told Death to be careful. Death assured her, "It won't be my blood."

Delia plopped another slice of pie on his plate. Death said he couldn't eat another bite. Delia pulled a pistol, cocked it and held it against Death's skull: "Eat the pie, skeleton boy." Death quickly ate the pie and let out a huge belch. Delia pitied William. He was the ugliest thing, all bones and pale skin. He looked like the rag doll her master's children left outside in the rain. *And the things he did with other men…!* The thought made Delia cringe.

Forever in need of funds to help newly freed slaves, Delia asked Death if she could paint his portrait to sell: no one knew what he looked like. Death said he intended to keep it that way, but he agreed to the creation of Captain Death dolls, so long as they came with a soft, cloth sword, or Rafe Naider the consumer advocate would have the dolls recalled; a sharp sword could put someone's eye out.

Delia excused herself to find Death a dark suit and some boots. Clancy poured himself more wine. When he leaned across the table to pour wine into Death's chocolate cup, Death put his hand over his cup, *no*. Clancy thought it odd, *but that's more wine for me!*

When Clancy had enough wine to make him brave, he blurted out:

"So…who are you really?"

Death blinked. The last person who had challenged his identity was Benjamin Franklin's grandson. Death was not forced to run the child through the liver, thanks to Dr. Franklin, who hushed his grandson by quoting himself: *Three can keep a secret, if two of them are dead.* Dr. Franklin happily kept Death's secret: why interfere with someone doing such good deeds? Just as Death checked authority, Franklin would check Death. He would expose Death at the appropriate time, after Death succeeded in emancipating all slaves, and then turned on him for opening and reading mail, and being a bigger hypocrite than Thomas Jefferson (Franklin's "rules" drove

Death up the wall: "*Rarely use venery but for health or offspring* said London's busiest ladies' man who had only three children; *Dine with little, sup with less: do better still, sleep supperless* said the man who obviously never, ever missed supper; *Early to bed and early to rise*…the doctor never saw a sunrise in his life!" Death could have gone on for hours).

Clancy smiled. "My father lost a drinking contest to Captain Death…thirty-five years ago. Are you telling me you outdrank my father – two years before your father met your mother? You must have been one precocious little sperm."

Death instinctively reached for his rapier.

Clancy poured himself another glass of wine. "Tell me the story! This, I have to hear…"

Death released the grip on his rapier. "When I was five years old, my father knew what I was, and dumped me in an orphanage. When the orphanage knew what I was, they dumped me in the Royal Navy. When I was fourteen, an English privateer sailed past us at Dover. They said the captain's name was William Death. I jumped ship and swam to his when I saw the name of his ship: the *TERRIBLE*. 'Captain Death?' 'The *TERRIBLE?*' What boy could resist?

"Two months later, we were attacked by the French privateer *VENGEANCE*. They killed everyone, except me. Captain Death said when he died, I could take his name…if I could live up to it."

Clancy poured another drink and laughed. "Am I the only person who read the reports of Captain Death's death in fifty-six?"

"The public has no memory!" said Death "Do they remember anything Rafe Naider did for them?"

"You started with nothing. *Nothing*. And look what you've accomplished."

"Yes, a great success. Slavery is still legal, women have almost no ownership rights, and our little recent uprising in London…I managed to get fifty-five innocent people hanged, drawn and quartered. My crew…you saw them, lined up on the dock, tossed into a wagon. Everywhere I go, I leave a trail of wreckage.”

Where had Clancy heard that before? For a moment, Death looked like he might cry. He then sat up straight. “I dread joining the Sons of Liberty, a group of thugs who are such cowards, they disguise themselves as Indians and don’t have the guts to dump tea into Boston Harbor in broad daylight. But I can no longer find volunteers. I’ve gotten fifteen crews killed. That’s more than most British naval captains.”

“Rafe Naider!” said Clancy. “We find *JUSTICE* and join Naider’s Raiders!” Surely, Naider would finally make Clancy a Raider for recruiting Captain Death!

Death growled, “Rafe gave me fifty pounds to study law with George Wythe. I took the money, bought ten kegs of gunpowder, blew up a plantation house, set fifty slaves free and settled them up North. Was Rafe impressed?”

“He sued you.”

“He sued me! Besides, Rafe won’t let me kill anyone, and I’m too old to let my talents go to waste. Rafe is right on one count: saving lives is fun. Alas, to save lives, one has to kill a few bullies.” Death finished his chocolate and sighed.

“Excellent shops in Boston,” said Clancy, for he didn’t know how he could possibly top Death’s story. “I shall stroll into each one wearing my embroidered coat, open lines of credit and default on every payment.” Clancy took a drink, grinned, and looked at Death.

Death was not grinning.

Death finally said, “I thought you fought at Culloden. They say you killed fifty Englishmen with a broadsword…or a butter knife…or a fork…or a teaspoon…or a napkin ring….”

“That was almost thirty years ago,” Clancy said as he poured another drink. He was too embarrassed to correct Captain Death: it was a sgian-dubh. His commanding officer had taken his rifle and sword and given them to soldiers who did not draw caricatures of Bonnie Prince Charlie.

Death said, “You’re not what I hoped to find. You are not your father.”

Clancy played an *A* on his wine glass. “We both had

romantic notions of what the other was like. You more than lived up to your end. Oh, well, I'm used to disappointing people..." Suddenly dizzy, Clancy rested his head on the table.

Clancy opened his eyes two seconds later, or so he thought, and was blinded by sunlight. A clock chimed noon. The dining table was wiped clean. His boots were gone. His new Masonic ring was gone...

...and so was Captain Death.

XIV
JOHN ADAMS FLIPS HIS WIG

Clancy was thankful that Captain Death, or whoever stripped him of his boots, at least left him the beautiful cream silk embroidered coat. Death had rejected it, saying it would attract too much attention. Clancy attracted plenty of attention as he strode along High Street in the coat and bare feet.

Clancy vowed to sober up, find Captain Death, and make a better impression. He feared for Death going alone to the Sons of Liberty. What might those pseudo-puritans do to a man like William Death?

Clancy checked for mail at Benjamin Franklin's post office. Clancy wrote hundreds of letters to people he admired, but between ships sinking, ships raided by pirates, post riders falling off cliffs, and post masters hanging onto letters to show to their friends for a good laugh, it was a miracle any of his letters reached their destinations. Clancy wrote in English, French, German, Spanish, Italian, Latin, Greek, Gaelic, and Algonquin, but his tendency to admire people on the run from the law didn't help him become a great man of letters. Still, the ever-optimistic Clancy always checked for mail.

There was no letter from Virginia or Scotland, but there was one from France (had Dr. Franklin gone over to the Frogs? Clancy hoped so – *Tell them I'll help them invade America if they promise to open some restaurants*). Upon seeing the scrawl, Clancy almost crumbled the letter, dismissing it as yet another drunken ramble from some admirer of his father, but, after much squinting, Clancy realized the shaky penmanship was possibly the result of old age, but more likely, in the case of its author, another type of drink. Voltaire was begging Clancy to send money again. Clancy grimaced: after lodge dues and taking care of his families, friends, neighbors, widows and orphans and the village idiot, there was rarely anything left.

Clancy could not make head nor tail of the rest of the letter, but presumed Voltaire was still campaigning on behalf of the serfs of Saint-Claude. The letter was undated, and Clancy hoped the matter was old and had resolved itself. He ripped several gold buttons off his silk coat and exchanged them for a sheet of paper, postage, and a ride on the express postal coach to New York. He wrote to Voltaire that he had received his request, would do his best to help the great author as soon as he found some shoes, and gently suggested Voltaire

lay off the coffee. Clancy was keen to make Voltaire a brother and worried the Freemasons would reject him for having an addiction that so unsteadied his hand he could not operate a pair of compasses, and they would lose a great brother. One could never tell what might induce the Freemasons to blackball a man.

Clancy worried about Sarah. If she were well, she would have sent him some sarcastic missive by now: *having wunderfull time with Hunting Bare he is a far bettir man then you and Hung like a Horse and lasts All Night Long.* On the coach to New York, Clancy scoured the Philadelphia gazettes for messages. There was one from Gowan No Last Name: *Just got out of jail again. Yr wife, children gone. Rumor Mill says they are with Shawnee. Behave yrself. – G. NLN.* For once, Clancy hoped the Virginia Rumor Mill was right.

Clancy ran out of gold buttons twenty miles short of Boston. As he walked north, he saw, above the tall trees swaying in the December wind, a lightning rod. A five-story house, here, in the middle of nowhere? Then he saw the ship's mainmast.

He walked through the woods to an inlet, and found, perched on a sandbar, a brigantine named *JUSTINE*. The *N* was newer and whiter than the other letters, and sun-bleached wood made the ghostly remains of the old *C* behind the *N* visible. Did some Raider fresh out of Harvard really think this would fool their enemies? Was their new ship's carpenter only able to carve letters with straight lines? What the hell was Rafe Naider thinking?

n the great cabin, walls lined with bookcases, John Adams, a lawyer and delegate to the recently adjourned Continental Congress, stood on tiptoes so he could see Rafe Naider sitting at his desk, barricaded behind stacks of papers. Areebah guarded the door. Naider and Adams were both New England men, but Connecticut and Massachusetts were not the same country. Adams was not one to sit around and wait for George III to reject Congress's feeble, begging assertion of their rights and liberties.

"Parliament will see reason soon enough, Mr. Adams," Naider said between penning lawsuits.

"Parliament will only see the justness of our cause when we have our own fleet," Adams growled. "*JUSTICE* – or rather, *JUSTINE* – has the capacity to carry guns. Remove your library, Captain Naider, and arm her!"

Naider raised an eyebrow. "Move my library where – Benedict Arnold's bookstore? I don't trust him. If the colonists are allowed to appoint their own governors, and if town meetings are allowed–"

Adams flipped his wig – across the room and out the window. "Allowed? ALLOWED? The time for begging and endless talk and debate is over. Join Samuel Adams and the Sons of Liberty. Join Colonel Washington!"

"Join Captain Death!" someone chirped in the distance.

Adams turned, and saw Clancy climbing through the window, the ponytail of Adam's flipped wig between his teeth.

Adams went up to Clancy and took back his wig.

"You're out of jail, Mr. Redbeard. You found a better lawyer."

"I found a better crowbar. Captain Death is en route to Boston to join the Sons of Liberty."

Areebah groaned. "Just what our cause needs: a Massachusetts mob led by a homicidal berserker."

Adams said, "Mr. Redbeard, I would advise you to persuade Captain Death not to go near The Sons of Liberty." Adams turned to Naider. "William Death may be..." Adams pondered how to put it, "...romantically disoriented, but he has the experience to lead an American fleet. It would be wise to recruit him." Adams marched to the door. "There is no escaping the inevitable, Captain Naider. Join, or die!"

Clancy bowed. "My best to Abigail."

Adams stopped and turned, but before he could ask Clancy how he knew his wife, Areebah slammed the door in Adams' face.

Clancy bowed to Naider. "And my best to your new lady, *JUSTINE*. I hear, in France, the Marquis de Sade is writing a novel of that name. Very scandalous. In the end, he kills his heroine with a bolt of lightning." Clancy winked at Areebah.

"Why aren't we moving?" Naider asked Areebah.

"We're stuck on a sandbar, Dad! Do we send for help?"

"There are spies everywhere. We wait for rain."

"Wait not for the heavens to lift you out of this inlet," Clancy said. "*God helps those that help themselves.*"

"Spare us the Franklinisms," Areebah said.

"Algernon Sidney beat Franklin to that one by thirty-eight years," Naider corrected his daughter. Areebah stomped on Clancy's foot as she walked out.

"His Rotundancy is right," Clancy said to Naider. "What you need are guns. The *JUSTICE* has a peaceful reputation. Use that reputation to quietly sail alongside British warships and blast them out of Boston Harbor."

"You have been consorting with William Death."

"Aye, but we made no music together."

Naider showed Clancy a broadside: *REWARD for the Capture of THE BASTARD OF REDBEARD by the CHURCH for ROBBERY and ASSAULT...*

Normally, Clancy would have spent at least a week arguing with Naider, but he was behind in his drinking. Clancy went to the window. "Best wishes to you and *JUSTINE*. But take it from a much-married man: all women secretly want men to fight."

"Next time you see Dr. Franklin, tell him to cease sales of his bifocals," Naider said, looking at a contract's small print with a magnifying glass. "He'll put someone's eye out."

"How did you know I saw–" Clancy stopped himself from finishing that foolish question. Rafe knew everything.

Naider whispered, "Do you have any swag to spare?"

"Alas, I have not fallen over any rich people." And with that, Clancy jumped out the window.

Naider took out a knife, cut a new quill and called after Clancy, "Tell William Death he owes me fifty pounds!"

Clancy skipped into the first tavern he found and asked for a bottle of whisky. Clancy rummaged through his pockets, then took off his now buttonless silk coat and placed it on the table as payment. "I'll have no need of this. The whisky will keep me warm–"

"Redbeard!" said a man behind Clancy.

Clancy instinctively lifted his hands over his head in surrender. "As you can see, I am not a chip off the old block – merely a splinter." For which of his many crimes was he wanted here? Oh, that little church matter… Clancy turned around to face his accuser. It was Roderick's lemon-faced secretary. He was smiling.

"Your nephew and niece are home from school, and eager to meet their Uncle Clancy!"

The secretary must have drunk an entire bottle for him to be so friendly. Wasn't whisky wonderful!

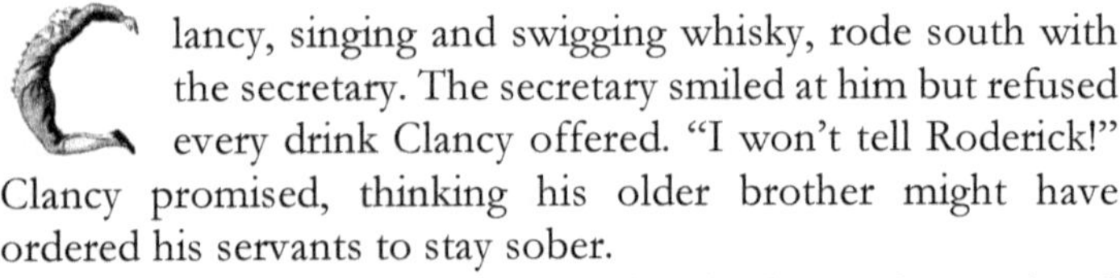

lancy, singing and swigging whisky, rode south with the secretary. The secretary smiled at him but refused every drink Clancy offered. "I won't tell Roderick!" Clancy promised, thinking his older brother might have ordered his servants to stay sober.

Clancy sang: *"In Williamsburg there lived a maid – mark well what I do say! Her eyes were red, her cheeks were brown, her curly hair was hanging down, I'll go no more a-rovin' with you fair maid…"*

Two armed servants followed close behind.

After ten days' hard riding, they arrived at Roderick's plantation, just in time for Christmas. Clancy rolled off his horse, and Roderick's slaves opened the doors. Pickled Clancy skipped in.

"Oh, Brother! Aunt Anne! Where are my nephew and niece? The prodigal bastard has arrived—"

Clancy tripped, fell flat on his face, and was knocked out cold.

XV
CLANCY OF CULLODEN

When Clancy woke at the strike of ten that night, he found himself being dragged by two orderlies down the public hospital's corridor and into a barred cell. They had stripped him of everything but his breeches. They put him in manacles chained to the wall.

"Gentlemen, where is my brother? Please send for my brother–"

The first orderly punched Clancy in the mouth. The second orderly, a kindly doctor who reluctantly joined the hospital staff after his home practice had mysterious burned to the ground, winced. The orderlies left. Howls and cries echoed down the corridor.

Clancy needed a drink. It had been, since his last, an entire day? His hands shook. He tried to remember what he did the last time he was alcohol-deprived…but he couldn't remember a time when he was. He always kept a stash, or he kept close to taverns. He once abandoned his war party when the liquor ran out. It was a wise decision: while he was in a tavern drinking, the other men were all slaughtered.

Clancy saw an old man in the cell opposite him. "Hello. I'm Clancy."

There was no reply.

"Are you from Virginia? I was born somewhere in the Mediterranean. Mother was a bit hazy. Father kidnapped her from her tribe and kept her drunk most of the time. Speaking of which, do you have anything to drink? Not water, I mean…"

The old man was silent. Clancy saw, in the cell next to the old man, poking through the bars, a woman's long silver and pepper hair.

"Mary…! Mary…Mary, why did you have me arrested for bigamy?"

Mary groaned, "Your brother…"

"Why are you here? The Raleigh Tavern said you went off with a widower."

"Your brother…your brother…"

Of course, it was Roderick. Why had he dared venture onto the same continent as his brother? How many people died as Roderick tried to get to him? The young pockmarked jail guard…Calvin, whose call to the women at the gallows saved his contemptible life…his son Patrick – was he really decapitated by a low-hanging branch? His wife and daughter in Scotland – was it Roderick who poisoned the well? The black boy with the oriental eyes – the charming letters the boy wrote thanking him for his support had ceased two years ago. Roderick probably learned of his existence and extinguished it.

There was a chorus of sobbing and moaning from the other cells. Clancy began singing:

"Let tyrants shake their Franklin Rod and slav'ry clank her galling chains! We fear them not, we trust in God! Virginia's God forever reigns…When God inspir'd us for the fight their ranks were broke their lines were forc'd, their ships were shatter'd in our sight or swiftly driven from our coast —"

The first orderly unlocked Clancy's cell.

"The foe comes on with haughty stride – sorry, I'll shut up–"

The orderly punched Clancy in the gut and walked out.

Clancy gasped for breath. He used to be able to take a punch easily. The years were catching up with him.

A woman's voice echoed off the brick walls: "Clancy…Clancy…you're rushing the beat…"

"Aunt Anne?!"

Aunt Anne had often told Clancy what a disappointment he was to her, failing to use his inherited skills. She, unlike Clancy, had been piratical for a few years with her chum Mary Read. Aunt Anne had famously told her lover, Calico Jack, as he begged her to rescue him from hanging, *if you'd fought like a man, you would not be hanged like a dog.* Clancy waited for Aunt Anne to say some variation of it to him, but she was silent. Clancy knew it was his fault she was here. She stood up for him at Roderick's party, and she was paying for it.

Clancy slipped his right hand out of the manacle. He yanked on his left manacle and pulled out the chain and a chunk of the wall. Clancy ran to the cell bars.

"Aunt Anne, where's Sarah?"

"Roderick," Aunt Anne mumbled from two cells down the corridor. "Roderick. Roderick…"

"Aunt Anne! Where are my children?"

"God help them…for you can't."

The orderlies came and chained Clancy to the cell bars, with his back to the corridor. The first orderly stood guard outside, whittling a block of wood.

Clancy said, "Please, tell my wife that I love her."

The first orderly poked his knife through the bars and cut the back of Clancy's hand. Clancy winced. "I appeal to you, as a man…please tell my wife I love her."

The orderly cut Clancy's other hand. Clancy silently mouthed; *please tell my wife I love her....*

Clancy was escorted down the corridor and into an examination room by the two orderlies. They locked Clancy into a chair with arm and leg restraints and left. Clancy shook – he didn't know whether from the cold, fear, or lack of alcohol. He saw bloodstains on the walls. On a table lay an assortment of medical instruments used for various incisions and extractions.

The Reverend Harrison entered, smiling, pushing a tea trolley with a cloth draped over what must have been the world's biggest teapot.

"Where's Doctor de Sequeyra?" Clancy asked.

"On holiday. But never you fear. I have much experience dealing with disturbed minds. How are we feeling, Clancy?"

"Much better! The orderly let me sleep for ten minutes last night. I feel wonderful – total recovery!"

The Reverend unveiled the tea trolley, revealing a device with a crank and a large glass jar.

"Is that Benjamin Franklin's famous turkey cooker?"

The Reverend cranked the electrostatic generator. "My, my, you have a very inquisitive, if highly unbalanced, mind. This will return you to your senses–"

The Reverend touched the discharge rod to Clancy's temple. Clancy convulsed. Blood poured out his mouth.

"Ah," said the Reverend. "Next time, try not to bite your tongue."

The Reverend put a bone in Clancy's mouth, which dropped right out.

"Bite down. Bite down. Good dog."

The Reverend shocked Clancy again, the charge creating a *CRACK!* as loud as a pistol shot. Clancy convulsed so violently that the Reverend had to grab the back of the chair to keep Clancy from capsizing.

The bone fell out of Clancy's mouth. "Death...is coming for me."

"You're in excellent health, Clancy."

"William Death...William Death will come for me."

"William Death was killed last year in South Carolina."

"No...we dined together in Philadelphia."

"In your mind, Clancy. In your mind."

Clancy was horrified. He had imagined having dinner with Captain Death for so many years, planning the stories and jokes he would tell him...was that night in Philadelphia just a dream? It would explain Death's sudden disappearance. But how did Clancy wind up in John Dickinson's house? And that silk coat – where was it? Had he ever left Virginia...?

The Reverend cranked the electrostatic generator.

"No –!"

The Reverend shocked Clancy again.

C lancy squatted on the floor of his cell, unmanacled. With one hand, Clancy stroked his hair, comforting himself. With the other hand, he played air musical glasses, quietly humming *Chester*.

T hat evening in the treatment room, the orderlies pushed Clancy up against a board, locked him in neck, wrist and leg restraints, and left him for an hour. Clancy was about to fall asleep when he heard someone coming down the corridor. A woman entered carrying a heavy bucket. Clancy smiled the best he could with blood caked on his lips. The woman sneered, went behind the board, and Clancy heard water being poured into a large tub. The woman went out, carrying the bucket with one finger. Clancy realized what was about to happen and screamed.

"OH GOD NOT THAT! ANYTHING BUT THAT! DON'T! NO, I'LL DO ANYTHING! DON'T, PLEASE DON'T!"

The Reverend came in, cheery as ever.

"Good evening, Clancy."

"Please...ever since I was a boy, I have had nightmares

about drowning. Hilarious, I know, for the son of a pirate. But I do not see any benefits arising from making my nightmares a reality."

The Reverend did not answer.

"I give up," Clancy said. "Tell me the way you want me to act. I can pass for normal, for short periods of time. Please, I can't bear being alone in that cell–"

The Reverend dunked Clancy back, submerging his head in the cold water. The Reverend tilted Clancy back upright. Clancy choked.

"Please...please, just kill me. Then Sarah can legally remarry, and my twins can have a new father. Please kill me. It's what my brother wants."

"Your brother wants you to be well, Clancy."

"My brother has wanted me dead since the day I was born! Put Roderick on this slab, show him what abuse is like, and cure him of mistreating those beneath him!"

The Reverend dunked Clancy. After a minute, he uprighted Clancy, and waited for him to catch his breath.

"Please, please, kill me..."

The Reverend whispered, "Where is Rafe Naider?"

Clancy grinned. "So that's what you want."

They wouldn't kill him. But if his twins still lived, it would not be for long. Roderick would bring them to the hospital and roast them alive before his eyes. Would he have the strength to sacrifice those dear innocents, for the sake of Naider's justice? Should he? Were Naider's Raiders finished? But if *JUSTICE* sank, how many other thousands of innocents would die? Clancy kept silent. The Reverend dunked him again.

The orderlies dragged Clancy down the corridor. As they passed one of the cells, Clancy saw strands of long nut-brown hair on the floor.

"Sarah! SARAH!"

Clancy grabbed the cell bars. The first orderly hit Clancy's hands with a club. Clancy saw an empty wine bottle next to Sarah's head.

"Take that bottle away! Sarah!"

The Reverend came to comfort Clancy. "It's part of her cure."

"It's killing her!"

The first orderly hit Clancy in the back.

"Let me hold her! I'm not letting go until I've held her! I'll tell you where Rafe Naider is."

The Reverend nodded to the orderly, and he unlocked Sarah's cell. Clancy ran to Sarah.

"Sarah…Sarah, my love..."

Sarah lay face down, motionless, a dried pool of vomit next to her head. Clancy turned her over. Lightning from a storm passing along the York River illuminated her face.

She had been dead for at least three days. With all the overflowing chamber pots in the hospital, it wasn't surprising no one smelled her rotting.

Clancy wiped crusted vomit off Sarah's cheek with his sleeve. With his fingers, he brushed her hair. He would make everything all right.

"Don't you worry, Sarah…" He sang, "*Farewell and adieu to you fair Irish lady. I'll go no more a-rovin with you fair maid…*"

At the far end of the corridor, there was screaming. The Reverend nodded for the two orderlies to stop it, and they did.

Clancy closed Sarah's eyes. He straightened her legs and folded her hands across her breasts. Several of her fingers were broken, as were her wrists.

The Reverend put his hand on Clancy's shoulder. "Come, Clancy. Tell us where Rafe Naider is, and you may go free."

Clancy put his hand on the Reverend's hand...and pulled the Reverend down on the floor. Clancy strangled the Reverend for a few seconds. And then he broke his neck.

The first orderly came into Clancy's cell. Clancy grabbed the wine bottle, broke it on the floor, and stuck the bottle end in the first orderly's jugular.

Mary, watching from her cell, smiled for the first time in months. The second orderly ran in, saw the dead orderly, and broke into a jig.

"Unlock Mary's cell," Clancy ordered.

The second orderly obeyed, and begged, "Take me with you!"

"Bring five horses and a wagon round back." Clancy smiled at Mary, "Pick the prettiest horse."

Clancy took the orderly's keys, unlocked all the prisoners' cells, and, lastly, Aunt Anne's. Aunt Anne faced the wall, mumbling incoherently.

Clancy said, "Anne Bonny."

Aunt Anne turned around and saw him.

"Clancy, The Red Warrior, lives."

"I have pulled myself together," said Clancy. "Come. We have work to do."

Anne Bonny fixed her hair and took Clancy's offered arm. Heads held high, they walked out.

Clancy, torch in hand, kicked open the front doors of Roderick's – or rather, his mansion.

"Oh, Brother, I'm home!"

Clancy tossed his torch under the drapes. The velvet caught fire.

The butler swung a silver tray at Clancy. Clancy grabbed the tray and bashed the butler over the head with it, knocking him to the floor.

Two guards ran into the entrance hall. Clancy grabbed a sword displayed on the wall and slashed the first guard's face, stabbed the second guard in the heart, then stabbed the first guard in the heart.

Clancy took the first guard's pistol, handed it to Mary and stood behind her.

"Just aim, and–"

BANG! Mary shot the guard charging down the stairs square in the chest. Clancy kissed her cheek.

"That's my woman! Get the carriage."

Clancy handed Mary the second dead guard's pistol, and Mary ran out the front door. The iron-burned unmusical redcoat came out of the library, brandishing a sword.

"Ah!" grinned Clancy. "My wife's savior, in the employment of my brother. I should have known."

The redcoat asked, "You think you can threaten the interests of the Crown, and live?"

"Uh, yes. A message from my wife–"

Clancy slashed the redcoat's throat. He dodged the spray of blood, which landed on the portrait of Governor Dunmore.

Clancy called, "Attention, everyone, attention!"

Four black slaves peeked out from the kitchen. Clancy picked up his torch and, as he spoke, set fire to all the drapes and tapestries.

"This is my house, willed to me by my father. As of this moment, I emancipate all slaves, who are under the impression they are the property of my brother when, in fact, you were willed to me. As the Virginia statute of seventeen twenty-three only allows men to emancipate their slaves in the case of meritorious service, I hereby declare that surviving one day in the service of my brother qualifies you all! Alas, as the courts of Virginia will certainly reject my argument, for only Governor Dunmore and his council may give the yea – and, in so ruling, will permit the church to scoop you up and sell you for their own profit – I suggest you gather your possessions…" Clancy grinned, "…my brother's possessions – gold, silver, small, easy to carry valuables – and meet me outside in ten–"

Clancy looked at the fast-moving flames.

"–three minutes."

The slaves and indentured servants ransacked the mansion. Clancy pulled off the dying iron-burned redcoat's boots. "Where is my brother?"

"North…"

"Why would Roderick go north?"

"William Death sank one of his slave ships."

Death lived! *He lived!*

"Where are my nephew and niece?"

"Smothered when Roderick realized they weren't his offspring."

Clancy nodded. He should have known.

"And my twins? Where are they?"

The iron-burned redcoat looked up as he died. Clancy looked up at the flames licking the ceiling.

Wearing the dead redcoat's boots, Clancy kicked opened the nursery doors. Clancy's twins, in bed, bolted up.

"Daddy's here!" Clancy announced.

His twins screamed, delighted by Daddy's wild appearance.

"And so is your Aunt Anne Bonny!"

Anne Bonny, a pistol in each hand, strolled past the doorway and shot two guards dead. The twins watched their father lift the end of their bed, pull back the rug, pry up one of the floorboards, and pull out a dusty cutlass inscribed *Blackbeard.*

Clancy carried his twins on his hips out of the burning mansion, Blackbeard's cutlass in a scabbard around his waist. Clancy put his children in the waiting carriage, opposite Mary.

"You're going to have new friends, and a new family, and even new names," Clancy smiled. "What fun you'll have. I wish I could stay with you forever…but I have to do something."

Two ex-slaves climbed into a wagon filled with swag. Anne Bonny came out of the mansion, carrying Clancy's portrait of his father over her head. Roderick's butler came up behind

Anne and grabbed the painting's frame. Anne pulled a pistol from her pocket and shot the butler dead.

Clancy took the painting from her. "Really, Aunt Anne, you are too sentimental," and he carried the painting back into the burning mansion.

In the entrance hall, Clancy tore the blood-splattered portrait of Governor Dunmore off the wall and hung his father's portrait in the governor's place. The wallpaper around the painting burned. Clancy took one last look at Father and left.

At the Shawnee winter camp, they initially waved them away. Four more mouths to feed? But when Anne Bonny fired her gun and, from a hundred fifty yards, blew the head off the squirrel that had terrorized the camp for months, the Shawnee welcoming committee came running. Clancy introduced his clan to his cousin, Hunting Bear, a middle-aged, muscular, handsome hunter. Mary and his children had never seen a man so glorious. Hunting Bear touched Mary's long silver-and-pepper hair and smiled, showing his terrible teeth. Mary's hair was nice, the way it caught the light, but he really liked how she held that rifle. Clancy's twins were polite and strong. Clancy Redbeard finally brought some good gifts. He wasn't such a useless selfish bastard after all.

Hunting Bear held out a cornhusk doll to Clancy's daughter. She took the cornhusk doll and dropped the doll

Clancy had given her on the ground.

Mary turned to kiss Clancy. Clancy turned away and said as he walked to the carriage, "Go, old whore. You bore me."

Mary, Aunt Anne and the twins walked away with their new family.

Clancy silently sobbed as he walked away from his life, hoping, if his family turned around, they would mistake his heaving sobs for mocking laughter, and think him an even bigger bastard than they'd imagined…and then think of him no more.

Clancy unharnessed the postilion horse from the carriage and galloped north, to the place of darkness. The lightning storm was so intense, it seemed to be daylight with momentary flashes of blackness, and Clancy was able to ride all through the night.

XVI
KNOCKING COMMON SENSE
INTO THOMAS PAINE

March 20, 1775

Kerrigan, the coffeehouse proprietor, refilled the gentleman's cup of chocolate, and noticed he was reading an anti-slavery article in the *Pennsylvania Journal* written by "JUSTICE." Kerrigan wondered who this 'Justice' was; Rafe Naider always signed his name.

The chocolate-drinking gentleman now made notations on a piece of paper. His elegant handwriting titled it *Wealthy*

Women Friends, and it was divided into columns of different towns. Under *Philadelphia,* he drew a little coffin next to the name *Deborah Franklin.* Now that Dr. Franklin's wife was safely dead, Mr. Kerrigan wondered if Ben would return to Philadelphia. His patronage could save his coffeehouse.

When Kerrigan took his flask from his pocket and went to pour a generous drop in the chocolate cup of his new special customer, the gentleman put his hand over his cup, *no.* Kerrigan was intrigued and tried to guess the gentleman's vocation. Surely, from his sobriety, this was no author! The gentleman had a sword, and two pistols, an aristocrat's bearings, but he wore a plain chocolate brown coat and breeches…a Quaker? A fighting Quaker? Or, a…

…PIRATE?

I should be so lucky! thought Kerrigan. It would be a nice change to have such an interesting man stay at his house. Those *Wealthy Women Friends* told an interesting tale…perhaps the gentleman would introduce him to one – "Are you in need of a position, sir?"

The gentleman had recognized the *Pennsylvania Journal* article's prose; the nom de plume confirmed the author's identity. On a fresh sheet of paper, the chocolate-drinking gentleman drew a man's portrait.

"No, I have one. I am going to kill my brother."

Kerrigan froze. He now had control over his money after his wife choked to death on a wishbone while berating him for buying her the wrong sort of birthday present (birthdays were for *special* gifts, like china, silver and gold jewelry, not *books).* After enduring twenty years of ear-shattering drama, he bought this quiet establishment so he could surround himself with authors who sat around all day reading gazettes and never tipped. Kerrigan had never met anyone with such subtle panache. Kerrigan then noticed that the bearded gentlemen had drawn little coffins next to all the women listed under *Annapolis, Baltimore,* and *Wilmington.* There were many names of yet-to-be encountered women in *New York, Newport, New Bedford,* and *Boston.* The gentleman appeared to be slaughtering his way up the East Coast.

Kerrigan leaned down and whispered, "Can I hire you to kill my mother-in-law?" for though The Screamer was dead, her mother yet lived.

Clancy continued his drawing. He wanted to get the nose just right. It was a fine line between an impressive nose and a comical one. "I must ensure the safety of my children, and other men's children. I do not expect to survive my task. Is this man in Philadelphia?"

Clancy held up his drawing. Kerrigan gasped.

"Please don't kill Tom," Kerrigan begged. "He's my only customer who tips."

In the back room of his bookshop, where he kept a printing press, Robert Aitkin crumbled a sheet of paper and threw it on the floor. "I am not publishing an essay on how families can make gunpowder in their own homes!" he shouted at his fifty-pounds-a-year executive editor of *Pennsylvania Magazine*. "What will you have women and their children making next? Musket balls? No more abolitionist essays – they don't sell! And enough with the humor and irony!"

A gold coin flew across the room and landed on the desk. Aitkin turned around and saw Clancy standing in the doorway.

Clancy said, "I would like to commission a pamphlet: an argument on hereditary succession, and the benefits of republicanism and declaring independence from our British masters that will stir the chocolate pot of public debate so violently, the consumer shall froth at the mouth."

The executive editor turned around. It was Tom Paine.

Tom had longed to leave Aitkin but couldn't find another position. After the Hutchinson Letters Affair, his only character reference lost its luster; if Dr. Franklin made private correspondence public, what god-awful thing might his protégé do? Tom would have gotten better-paying work had his letter of introduction been signed by The Bastard of Redbeard.

When he saw Clancy, Tom's jaw dropped.

Aitkin looked down his nose at Clancy. "For the safety of this journal and that of the public, there are two words I will not allow to be printed: *republicanism* and *independence*."

"Well, then," Clancy said. "I shall have to take your best author away from this cowardly publication and find another publisher. And Tom can write all the humor and irony he wants."

Tom walked past Aitkin, eyes glued to his savior.

Clancy smiled, "Pick up the money, Tom."

"Oh...!" Tom hurried back to Aitkin's desk and picked up the gold coin.

Tom clung to Clancy's arm as his rescuer escorted him to his new, quiet rooms above Kerrigan's coffeehouse.

"Fifty pages, Tom. We need to price your pamphlet so everyone can afford it. After the first printing sells out, renounce your copyright, and announce you're donating all royalties to the new American army to buy our soldiers..." Clancy tried to think of something appropriate, useful, and ironic.

"Mittens," suggested Tom, whose hands froze when he didn't have a quill in his hand.

"Warm hands, cold hearts," Clancy squeezed Tom's frosty writing hand. "We will treat the British as they have treated us. We are no longer subjects – we are verbs. Fifty pages. Make it funny!" Clancy wiped Tom's tears of joy with his sleeve.

Tom sobbed, "On the ship...out of my mind with fever...I thought you were a dream."

"I will soon be a nightmare. And Tom, try not to cry on the manuscript. One soggy letter could turn your revolution into simply another resolution, and we both know how useless Congress is."

There is nothing like having a pirate standing outside one's door to inspire an author to make a deadline.

Clancy reminded Tom that if America was to break away from England, they needed all hands on deck. Illiteracy was widespread; the pamphlet needed to be read aloud. "Fifty pages, Tom."

On the ninth of April, per their agreement, Clancy announced, "Time's up!" opened the door, and found Tom at his desk, bearded, unwashed, asleep, the completed pamphlet on his desk. It was five hundred pages long.

Why did he give Tom so much paper? Next time, if he wanted fifty pages, he would give Tom fifty pages! Still, it was one-fourth the length of his previous manuscript. The arguments were brilliant. And it was funny. *Good Tom!* Clancy brought Tom a cup of chocolate, but Tom fell asleep, so Clancy drank it, and spent all night and the next day writing up Tom's highlights in his beautiful calligraphy, until he had two forty-eight-paged pamphlets. Clancy wished he had time to think of a better title than *Common Sense.* Areebah would have titled it *George III is a Big Fat Idiot*, which would certainly sell, but it would also be easily dismissed. Comedy never got the respect it deserved. The colonists needed lawyers to take the pamphlet seriously and be seen reading it in plain view, not wrapped in brown paper. Clancy put one copy in his pocket, ready for the moment he met a courageous publisher, and had a post rider take the other copy to Henry Knox, a young bookseller in Boston.

Clancy flinched when he saw the name of the nearest tavern, but he took Tom's arm and strode straight into The London Bridge to secure pre-sales to keep his author housed and fed until he received other patronage. The tavern was packed with hard-working, hard-drinking men.

"Start spouting, Tom."

Tom lost his nerve when he saw the sea of large, carousing men. He took two steps back, towards the door.

"You're right, Tom: 'tis madness," smiled Clancy. "Let's just have a drink and drown our misery. Surely, tomorrow, the king will change his ways and treat us kindly. AFTER ALL," Clancy bellowed, and everyone in the tavern turned and looked at him, "we're all of English descent. 'Tis *our duty* to shake hands and cry *GOD SAVE THE KING.*"

"God save the king!" chorused the men, raising their glasses.

Steaming mad, Tom leapt onto a table –

"To say that reconciliation with England is our duty is truly farcical. The first king of England, of the present line, was a Frenchman; by that method of reasoning, England ought to be governed by France."

A small group of men laughed and wondered who this preacher was. Clancy nudged the man laughing the hardest, showed him the preview copy of *Common Sense*, and held out his hand. The man gave Clancy a coin, Clancy took his name and address and gave him a promissory note for a first edition – unsigned, to avoid a hanging for its seditious author.

Tom was on a roll: "Monarchy has laid the world in blood and ashes. To the evil of monarchy, we have added that of hereditary succession. One of the strongest natural proofs of the folly of hereditary right in kings is that nature disapproves it, otherwise, she would not so frequently turn it into ridicule by giving mankind an ass for a lion!"

A few men gasped, most laughed, one applauded.

"But it is not so much the absurdity as the evil of hereditary succession which concerns mankind. Men who look upon themselves born to reign soon grow insolent. Selected from the rest of mankind, their minds are early poisoned by importance, and the world they act in differs so materially from the world at large that they have but little opportunity of knowing its true interests."

Clancy heard someone behind him exclaim, "He's better than George Whitfield!"

Clancy spun around, and came face-to-face with Dr. Franklin, disguised in a false beard. It looked like the one Captain Death sported on the *LONDON PACKET*. In fact, it was the same beard (*HOW…?* Delia. She was forever reselling.

The beard had made two Atlantic crossings since supper at John Dickinson's). After Franklin's dressing-down in London over the Hutchinson Letters Affair, Franklin told everyone he would depart England in March, but had in fact sailed the very next day. He needed a few weeks to get settled in, unmolested, and contend with the pharaoh, get a thump on the head with Samson's jawbone, get right before the wind with all his studding sails out, and all his other two hundred-plus expressions for getting drunk. He was also avoiding Naider and his Raiders.

Clancy stuffed the coins and twenty addresses from pre-sales, and his copy of the forty-eight-paged pamphlet into Franklin's coat pocket.

"If it's not in print by winter…" Clancy said, squeezing Franklin's false beard in his fist.

Dr. Franklin's early-model bifocals fogged up and, as Naider had warned, the bottom halves popped out of their frames – though, luckily for Dr. Franklin, they fell not into but away from his eyes and broke on the floor.

"See?" Clancy grinned. "Rafe was right!"

Dr. Franklin almost lost his famous composure. "Naider needs to leave me alone and sue some *rich* men!"

"Poor Richard…by the way, I'm off to kill my brother."

"Thank God!"

"I suppose He will have a hand in it, though I shall lay the groundwork. And stop feigning to be Captain Death."

"Are you and William Death uniting?" Franklin rubbed his hands gleefully. "That will be like two rattlesnakes joining!"

Clancy strode towards the door. Franklin called out a well-meant axiom:

"Stoop, young man, stoop!"

Clancy's head hit a low beam. The beam splintered, and Clancy continued out the door without breaking stride. *Stoop as you go through the world, and you will miss many hard thumps.* For most men, carrying their heads too high did indeed bring many misfortunes. But Clancy was not most men. Clancy had spent his life stooping…but no more. Low-hanging beams would be wise to get out of his way.

Having gotten Tom on his feet and a quill in his hand, Clancy left Philadelphia. Mr. Kerrigan wept when he learned the chocolate-drinking pirate had left without supplying him the name of one – *not one!* – of his still-living Wealthy Women Friends, but was greatly cheered by the bag of gold coins equaling the amount it would have cost to replace Dr. Franklin's smashed armonica: *when you meet another honest man in similar distress, you must pay me by giving that sum to him.* Mr. Kerrigan paid off his mountain of debts and vowed to give unhappy authors free cups of chocolate forevermore.

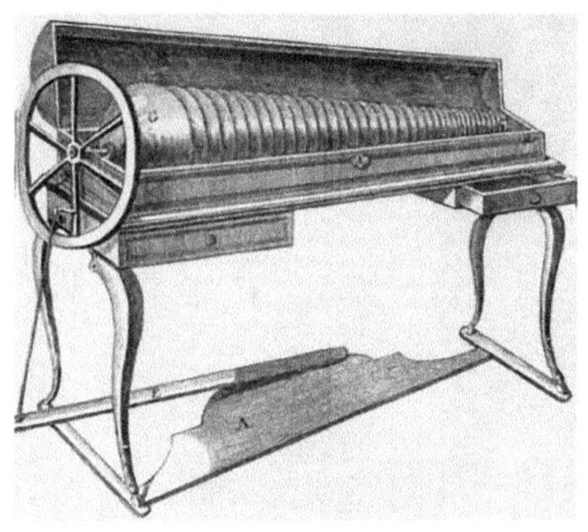

Clancy, on his second rented horse of the day, galloped north. He approached a group of young women. In the past, he would have stopped and chatted them up. He rode right past them, hearing Tom's voice in his head:

In England, a king hath little more to do than to make war and give away places, which, in plain terms, is to impoverish the nation. A pretty business indeed for a man to be allowed eight hundred thousand sterling a year for, and worshipped into the bargain!

Clancy rode on. Lightning lit the way.

Of more worth is one honest man to society and in the sight of God, than all the crowned ruffians that ever lived...

As Clancy rode out of New London, Connecticut, he passed a shop. In the window display stood three Captain Death dolls, with cloth swords. A sign in the window promised *"New Shipment Next Week!"*

XVII
PAUL REVERE'S TEAPOT

part from the sinking of Roderick's slave ship *Promised Land*, Captain Death's Boston mission was a colossal failure, and he was at the end of his rope. He wanted to die in the arms of, if not a lover, then a loving person. He hid in a cave by the shore for three days, unable to think of anyone he could trust –

Margaret.

Margaret was so kind to him on that voyage to England in seventy-three. She was the only reason he didn't scuttle the ship. Who could drown such a woman?

Over the years, he was whipped and flogged, and took five bullets and other abuses, but shirts and breeches kept the evidence hidden. He always ran in the opposite direction of smallpox epidemics, so managed to keep his face free of blemishes. Now, he either had to join Rafe Naider and work below deck, or get over his vanity, or die. He wondered if this terrible new scar would inspire fear. But when Margaret returned from church, went to her closet and found Death in it, mending his torn breeches, she failed to scream. She sent the servants and her children – she was pregnant with number nine – on a picnic, despite their protests that it was Sunday and what would the neighbors say, especially with her husband away hunting those terrorists Samuel Adams and John Hancock? Margaret opened her home and larder to the battered young pirate. Ever mindful that his mother died in childbirth, Death always made a special effort to help pregnant women, but Margaret insisted on waiting upon him; even with a baby kicking up a storm inside her, she was in far better health than Death. Margaret needed to get Death back on his feet. Trouble was brewing in Massachusetts.

The scar told a tale, though not one Death would ever want repeated. How could he have let those thugs take him by surprise? It took nine men, two for each limb and a fat one sitting on his chest to hold Death steady so the tenth could carve a large *S* into his right cheek, though number ten was so cowardly and in a hurry to attack and run he simply made three deep, crass slashes, insulting the eloquent curves of that most sensual of consonants. The last two men to let go of Death paid for it with their lives, but there were eight smug "Sons of Liberty" running around boasting of what they did. To get past this latest humiliation, Death needed a tremendous triumph. His scar would become not the brand of a social outcast but a trademark. It would be dashing and romantic. Countless men would engrave alphabetical characters into their flesh in emulation of Captain Death. He'd have to do something ridiculous, like lose a leg, wear an eyepatch and acquire a parrot to differentiate himself from his imitators.

Death sat in the sunroom, his feet up, drinking chocolate. It was delicious. He asked if he might have another cup? Margaret kissed his unscarred left cheek and went to the kitchen.

The previous day, Margaret visited Henry Knox's bookstore. Knox refused to read anything sent to him by some pirate's son in Philadelphia, but Margaret saw "An Englishman's" pamphlet in his woodpile, read it on the carriage ride home, and laughed so hard, snot flew out her dainty nose. *You must read it, William!* she insisted. The author was a genius, so intelligent and perceptive. It would give him encouragement. *All right*, said Death. As long as it wasn't written by that sickly twitchy big-nosed writer he saw on the *LONDON PACKET*. Death was too ashamed to admit the only words he knew how to read were *WANTED* (which only appeared once in the pamphlet), *REWARD* (which appeared not once), and *DEATH* (his name appeared three times!).

Paul Revere practiced recreating his pose: right hand on his chin, innocently glancing up at the imaginary audience that caught him contemplating the modestly magnificent craftsmanship of the silver teapot he cradled in his left hand. If customers recognized him from John Singleton Copley's portrait, the silversmith could double his prices.

Tensions were mounting in Massachusetts. Just last September, General Thomas Gage, the military governor, had taken all 250 half-barrels of gunpowder from the Provincial Powder House. "The Powder Alarm" made New Englanders come together like beads of mercury. There's one thing you never want to do to an American: threaten to take away his gun. New England was on the verge of full-scale war, when winter came and froze tempers, temporarily. But now it was spring.

Massachusetts would not be taken by surprise again. As a member of the Massachusetts Committee of Correspondence, Paul Revere arranged signals — one lantern in the Old North

Church bell tower if the king's troops came by land, two if by sea – and Revere would ride to Lexington to warn Samuel Adams and John Hancock, who were lying low at Reverend Clarke's country house. From their sources in London, the American Whig leaders knew of General Gage's orders to arrest Adams and Hancock before Gage himself did.

Dawes: cause, clause, claws, draws, gauze, gnaws, jaws, laws, paws, saws, vase...

Prescott: Bess, dress, fess, guess naught, guess not, less, mess, yes...

Bought, caught, dot, fought, got, hot, jot, lot, not, naught, ought, plot, rot, wrought, sought, sot, yacht, Less Scot, Guess Wot? Chamber pot –

CHAMBER POT! Tee hee hee! Revere tittered at how few words rhymed with his fellow express riders' names. His immortality was secure! Besides, Samuel Prescott was out of the running for inclusion in family-friendly poems: the not-so-good doctor would most likely be returning from his lady friend's house at the unwholesome hour of one a.m. (*The regulars are coming, and so am I!* It was a popular joke amongst Concord women that the militia were called minutemen because that's how long they lasted.) And William Dawes? His jittery horse would throw him at the first owl hoot. And neither man had a mistress who commissioned John Singleton Copley to paint *their* portraits. Yes, History would easily dispense with Prescott and Dawes. *Wheeeeeeeeeeeeee!*

While Revere pondered his teapot and whether he should prepare for the impending war or have dinner first, Clancy threw open the door. He did not give three loud knocks; he simply charged into the shop and slapped his list of *Wealthy Women Friends* on Revere's polished table.

"Know you these women?"

"*Know?*" leered Revere.

"Their whereabouts."

Revere ran his fat finger down the list. "You've become very organized, Redbeard..." Revere's finger stopped at the first *K.* "Margaret Kemble? You're joking."

"Ahhhhh, Margaret..." Clancy sighed at the memory of that wonderful evening.

Revere was appalled that The Bastard of Redbeard should be acquainted with such a fine lady. "Margaret Kemble *Gage*."

As in General Gage?! Clancy pocketed the list and snatched the teapot from Revere's hand.

"For recommending John Adams be my lawyer."

Clancy put the teapot under his arm and left.

Clancy rode through the countryside towards a house. Tom Paine's words sounded in his soul:

There is more to dread from a patched-up reconciliation than from independence. I protest that were I driven from house and home, my property destroyed, and my circumstances ruined, that as a man, sensible of injuries, I could never relish the doctrine of reconciliation...

Clancy slipped Blackbeard's cutlass through the crack between the door and the jamb, and lifted the latch. He pushed the door open with the tip of the sword, hoping to impress any children he encountered with a bit of braggadocio, but the house was devoid of little ones.

Margaret Kemble Gage was a year past forty. From the

parlor doorway, Clancy watched the aristocratic woman, with her beautiful large belly, arranging three flowers on a tea tray. *She remembers my Ikebana lessons!* thought Clancy. *She must have feminine company. No man would appreciate such artistry.*

"Margaret."

When she heard that unforgettable voice, her mouth fell open. Margaret spun around and saw a man who resembled Clancy Redbeard. It couldn't be – this man was sober and walking in a straight line.

Clancy said, "You're as beautiful as ever. But marrying a mere general? Really, Margaret, you can do better than that–"

As Clancy was about to slip his tongue into her open mouth, someone in the adjoining room, in a most unladylike fashion, belched. Clancy took the tea tray from Margaret and gave her his biggest smile. Then he glared down at the porcelain teapot, disgusted. It would not fetch as much as silver.

Clancy went into the sunroom and saw a man sitting with his back to him, thumbing through a pamphlet. He could see the man's left leg, and wondered why the general's leg was so skeletal, and his breeches so mussed.

"Enjoying the pamphlet, darling?" Clancy cooed to the general.

The man slammed the pamphlet shut when he heard the sudden change in pitch of Margaret's voice. Clancy saw the pamphlet's title page: *Common Sense.*

Clancy cooed, "I hope it's quite convinced you to leave America."

"Au contraire, mon cher, I am more determined than ever to stay," the man cooed back.

Clancy put the tea tray on a table and picked up the teapot. "Darling, I thought, since we weren't invited, we'd have our own little Boston tea party."

Clancy smashed the teapot against the wall – and a dark brown liquid came flying out. At first, Clancy thought it was Voltaire's favorite beverage, but when it took too long to drip down the walls, Clancy knew who had come to tea. Or rather, chocolate.

The man put his stockinged feet on the floor, turned, and William Death showed his profile to Clancy.

"My boots didn't fit?" asked Clancy.

"I easily filled them," replied Death, pointing to Clancy's boots resting by the fireplace.

"You sank my brother's ship. That was my task."

Clancy circled round Death, and saw his black eye, the cuts on his neck, and the scar.

Clancy squinted. "Is that a backwards Z, or two? I presume you did that to yourself in the mirror – as though you could tear yourself away from one for five minutes."

Death grinned. "If your vision is failing, or you've grown too senile to remember your *ABCs*, perhaps it's time to retire – permanently."

Death stood. Margaret ran in.

"Oh, it's an *S*," smiled Clancy. "For *Sons of Liberty*."

"I prefer *sodomite*," said Death, whipping out his rapier.

Margaret ran to Death. "William dear, don't hurt him – he's drunk again."

"William dear, he's sober," purred Clancy.

"God help us, he is," Margaret marveled. "William, go and rest – you've had too much chocolate."

"Please wait in the parlor, my dear," Death smiled at Margaret and gave her a gentle kiss on the cheek. "While Fancy Clancy and I settle our differences."

As Margaret walked past Clancy, he grabbed her waist, bent her over, and gave her a long, wet, no-holds-barred swashbuckling kiss.

It seemed to go on for hours. Death yawned and put on Clancy's boots. Death cleared his throat. He hummed the shanty *Farewell and Adieu*. With his rapier, he rapped the table's leg to get Clancy's attention. Finally, Clancy removed his tongue and let Margaret go. Margaret retired to the parlor, knocking over a vase as she staggered out. *Vive le France!*

Clancy drew his cutlass.

"You shouldn't have left me in Philadelphia," said Clancy

as he and Death circled tea table. "I do not like being abandoned."

"Well, then, Chocolate Nose," Death said. "You should have heeded Dr. Franklin's advice: *early to bed and early to rise makes a man healthy —*"

Death picked up a gold snuff box from the table and pocketed it.

"*—wealthy—*"

Death pocketed the silver teaspoons.

"—and able to buy enough gunpowder to blow the Royal Navy out of Boston Harbor."

Clancy pulled a canvas bag from his coat pocket. "*Many foxes grow grey, but few grow good.*" Clancy held the blade of his cutlass between his teeth, picked up a candlestick and stuck it in his swag bag.

"*Rebellion against tyrants is obedience to God,*" Death said as he stuck his rapier through the wire loop holding up a portrait of General Gage, lifted it, and caught the painting as it fell.

"John Singleton Copley, what a whore," sneered Clancy. "He'll paint anyone for a penny."

"Why doesn't Copley paint us?" sneered Death as he kicked the canvas out of its gold frame and broke the frame into easy-to-carry pieces.

Death sheathed his rapier and took something off a chain around his neck. He walked up to Clancy and held out his hand. Clancy saw it was the Masonic ring, with the square and compasses and skull, the one Death had given, and taken from him in Philadelphia.

Death wrapped his arms around Clancy and buried his face in the older man's neck. Clancy could feel Death's shoulder blades and spine jutting through his thin-skinned back. Clancy did not embrace Death as tightly as he longed to, for fear the boy might shatter in his arms.

Clancy and Death realized someone had entered the room. They quickly released one another, and prepared to pull their weapons, when they saw it was Margaret, stuffing the silver sugar pot and creamer into Clancy's bag.

"Men," Margaret gritted her teeth. "Emotional babies! Must women do everything?"

Clancy asked, "Margaret, dear, where is your silverware?"

"Er, ah–" Guilt-ridden Death pulled his overflowing swag bag from behind the sofa. He looked at Margaret, shrugged and smiled apologetically.

"Have you heard any news of my brother?" Clancy asked Margaret.

"No, thank goodness. My husband's troops are going to seize the munitions in Concord."

"Where are Naider's Raiders?"

"There's been no word of them for months...did you hear what I said about my husband's troops?" These men *never* listened. "They're going to arrest John Hancock and Samuel Adams!"

"Good," said Death, pocketing the last of the biscuits.

"You must warn them!"

"Tell Paul Revere to get off his fat ass, get on his horse and take a midnight ride," said Clancy. "We have some fundraising to do, some arms to procure, and then young Captain Death and I–"

Death turned and looked at Clancy.

"–are going to sea."

Death jumped up and down on the sofa with glee. Clancy pulled a Captain Death doll from his pocket and handed it to Margaret.

"Better than the real thing – won't go running off."

Clancy took his swag, and Margaret's copy of *Common Sense*, and ran out the back door. Death leapt off the sofa, picked up his swag bag, and went to Margaret, hanging his head – she thought so she could kiss his forehead. She brushed aside his beautiful forelock and kissed his forehead. He sighed and pointed to the gold locket around Margaret's neck.

"Oh..." Margaret reached around to remove her locket. Death put his arms around her and unhooked it for her. He kissed her neck softly and gave her a gentle hug. She smelled wonderful, like roses. She was so soft and warm. He could have held her forever –

"DEATH!" Clancy yelled from the doorway.

Death pecked Margaret on the cheek, grabbed his swag and ran after Clancy.

Clancy and Death ran as fast as their bags of swag would allow, Death skipping through the grass like a child.

"*Captain Death*," Clancy smirked. "What do all those little hugs and pecks on the cheek get you?"

Death twirled the locket of General Gage and grinned.

Clancy grinned. "Oh, women of Boston, look out."

XVIII
GEORGE WASHINGTON'S
BIGGEST MISTAKE

I n July, a tailor from Virginia told Clancy that the tailor's wife's friend's brother's wife's friend's sister's cousin heard a rumor that Governor Dunmore had abandoned Williamsburg and was living on a warship near Yorktown — with Roderick. Employing his various fleets, Roderick could terrorize the entire East Coast. Clancy berated Death for making such a show of sinking Roderick's slave ship. Did Death make it seem like an accident, as though the ship hit a hidden reef? *Nooooooo*, he had to take the credit, carving on a large rock by the shore, *Here Captain Death Sank Roderick Redbeard's Nefarious Slave Ship* Promised Land, *January 1, 1775* (the illiterate Death hired a fellow Freemason to do the inscription). Now Roderick had his guard up. Clancy figured Parliament's tactic was to conquer by dividing the colonies, North and South, and Roderick was just the man for the job.

Clancy asked Death if he received any of the 485 letters he sent him. Death said just one – a message in a bottle he found in Annapolis Harbor – and when he asked his newly-hired first mate to read it to him, he told Death it was from a young lady who wanted to give him money, and to please meet him in an empty storehouse at the edge of town – where the first mate and his friends robbed Death, beat him and left him for dead. A woman who found Death took him home, nursed him back to health, and read Clancy's admiring letter to him, in which Clancy asked, for the 485th time, to join his crew (giving Rafe Naider as a character reference), and signing it, "The Bastard of Redbeard." Death asked Rafe Naider about Clancy, and Naider said Death should take Clancy up on his offer: Clancy could read and write in nine languages and told great jokes...*oh, and he fought at Culloden.*

Unable to find Naider or Roderick, Clancy and Death presented themselves and their prizes to the general of the brand-new Continental Army, George Washington. Although pleased, Washington didn't want to be seen encouraging their methods. He took their booty, of course, but never got around to signing the orders granting them commissions and full pardons for theft, missing church (for Clancy. Death never missed a Sunday), and murder. Killing men simply because they wouldn't free their slaves? And killing a clergyman, even one found with three of his parishioners' missing gold watches and a crucifix in his pocket? If these pirates had no qualms about killing those men, how easily would they dispense with a slave-owning general?

The general kept a squinted eye on the pirates. In the evenings, when Washington presumed they would get drunk or engage in other debaucheries, The Bastard of Redbeard taught Captain Death to read and write. Clancy said that words were deadlier than swords, and books were better than shields

– they even stopped musket balls (though cannonballs tended to tear right through them), and Clancy worked Death hard night after night, patting him on the back as the young man continuously burst into tears of frustration, until Death could take dictation and read the bible and *Common Sense* aloud with confidence. Washington thought William Death might make a fine aide or dispatch rider…but The Bastard of Redbeard?

It was Clancy's idea to bring the cannon captured at Fort Ticonderoga to Boston and blast the British out of the harbor: "The guns have been sitting there since May – let's go fetch them!" Washington thought it madness. It was three hundred miles through the Berkshire Mountains! "So?" asked Clancy. "You're too busy attending balls to sign the order?" (Death clamped his hand over Clancy's big mouth and kissed their commissions adieu.) When Henry Knox overheard the idea and presented the plan as his own, it suddenly became a stroke of genius. Death exploded, and told Clancy, "Washington treats you like a woman!"

That his idea to bring the guns to Boston worked encouraged Clancy, even if the fat bookseller got all the credit. "Foxy Knoxy" tried to assuage his guilt by offering Clancy a keg of wine. Clancy asked for Knox's company's ration of chocolate instead. Clancy confessed to Death that, for most of his life, alcohol had clouded his judgment: the whisky after The Battle of Culloden, the rum after The Battle of Monongahela, the Madeira before, during, and after The Battles of Fiona, Polly, and Sarah... Death said the original Captain Death made him stop drinking when he joined the crew of the *TERRIBLE*, when he was a grog-soaked fourteen-year-old, and he hadn't had a drop since.

Sober Clancy began to think: the British had evacuated Boston and gone to Halifax, but would soon go for New York, an island that would easily fall to the Royal Navy. Clancy tried to warn Washington about Roderick, who would, without doubt, fortify his estates in New York, Philadelphia, and Baltimore, supply the Royal Navy, inflict significant damage against local militias and the Continental Army, and thwart any navy John Adams could muster. Clancy waited three months, but a pirate standing outside his tent did not inspire the general.

Clancy knew he was holding Death back. Rather than being impressed that Clancy Redbeard was the friend of Captain Death, Washington wondered why Captain Death had such low standards for friends. Clancy packed his things and instructed Death to tell Washington that the only reason Death had spent so much time in Clancy's company was because he needed a cheap penmanship instructor, and what a sot The Bastard of Redbeard was and how glad he was to be rid of that do-nothing. Death would have a magnificent career in Washington's army, and once Clancy was gone, Washington would certainly take Death's advice: "The general will never trust me. No one ever will," said Clancy. With that, he left.

A mile outside Washington's camp, while walking as quickly as he could, Clancy felt someone hook their arm around his. It was Death, his belongings slung over his shoulder. Death walked alongside Clancy, looking straight ahead.

"I trust you," said Captain Death.

Clancy knew he should order Death to return to Washington…but though he tried, he could not stop clutching Death's arm. Clancy started singing so he would not burst into tears. And so, Captains Redbeard and Death went to "borrow" some horses.

Washington soon regretted Clancy and Death's departure. Money and supplies promised by Congress failed to appear, and the militia were not worth the bread they ate. The pirates, on the other hand, had returned to camp every evening laden with provisions voluntarily handed over by cheerful ladies. Washington's soldiers, on the other hand, annoyed local civilians, plundered, defected to the British, stole military supplies, and were cowards under fire, constantly drunk, completely devoid of humor and good fireside stories, sang out of tune, and smelled like sheep. The pirates might have been cheeky, and local women might produce unnatural numbers of red-headed children that would be attributed to Washington (for hair color was the one trait he and Clancy shared)…but my God, *they got things done!*

Death reminded Clancy he had said, at Margaret's house, they were going to sea. Clancy promised they would, when they knew where the hell Rafe Naider and Roderick were. Clancy and Death went to New York City and, posing as violin dealers recently arrived from Cremona, inquired if Roderick Redbeard still owned that once-splendid Tudor house overlooking the Hudson? Nay, he had sold it. Roderick was probably liquidating old assets to buy more ships. Clancy scratched Father's oldest estate off the list and breathed a huge sigh of relief. Had Roderick armed that house, he could have blockaded the entire Hudson.

Clancy and Death set out that afternoon for Roderick's house south of Philadelphia, perfectly located for the British to arm, blockade the Delaware, and attack Congress — which might not be that bad an idea, Clancy thought. It might motivate Congress to get off their arses and do something. When Clancy and Death stabled their horses for the night, the groom told them he heard a rumor that Rafe Naider had shelled Philadelphia, killed the Johns Adams and Hancock, and made himself President of Congress. Clancy and Death spent the rest of the night roaring with laughter at the thought. War is a terrible thing, but it produces terrific stories.

January 1776

Preoccupied with settling into his house on High Street, playing with his grandchildren, and catching up on sleep during sessions of the Second Continental Congress, it had taken eight months for Benjamin Franklin to find a publisher for Tom Paine's pamphlet. *Common Sense* quickly became the best-selling pamphlet in history, and the most pirated, with every publisher engaging in pre-war profiteering by printing their own "special edition" and keeping the profits for themselves. When Death realized the pamphlet was written by that sickly twitchy big-nosed man on the *LONDON PACKET*, he laughed – and then exploded when he learned Clancy had commissioned it – THIRTEEN MONTHS AGO. Why hadn't Clancy the common sense to print the pamphlet himself, and use the proceeds to create his own navy? They would have won the war already! Clancy sighed, "Oh well, live and die – uh, *learn*." Frustrated beyond words, Death swore he would never speak to Clancy again. His vow lasted twenty minutes, when he got lonely and wanted to hear Clancy's joke about the doctor, the lawyer, and the priest: *a ship hits an iceberg and the doctor says, "Get the women and children ashore!" The lawyer says, "Fuck the women and children!" and the priest says, "Is there time?"*

At Franklin's post office, there was money waiting for Clancy from Virginia: *Royalties from Common Sense Williamsburg Edition.* The note was signed *Gowan Pamphlet.* Clancy liked Gowan's new last name. Clancy and Death invited themselves to stay at John Dickinson's empty house while Dickinson was serving in the Pennsylvania militia. Dickinson has seen the light – or the end of Delia's gun – and she had been freed. Death was happy for Delia but sighed when he opened the pie-free larders. There was still no Franklin Rod on Dickinson's house, a wrong Clancy corrected in two hours.

COMMON SENSE:
ADDRESSED TO THE
INHABITANTS
OF
AMERICA,
On the following interesting
SUBJECTS.

I. Of the Origin and Design of Government in general; with concise Remarks on the English Constitution.

II. Of Monarchy and Hereditary Succession.

III. Thoughts on the present State of American Affairs.

IV. Of the present Ability of America, with some miscellaneous Reflections.

Written by an ENGLISHMAN.

Man knows no Master save creating HEAVEN,
Or those whom choice and common good ordain.
THOMSON.

PHILADELPHIA, Printed.
And Sold by R. BELL, in Third-Street, 1776.

On July second, Congress finally did something, and two days later, presented to the world a declaration that the United States of America was Independent from Great Britain. Clancy thought the document rather dry, and that they had picked the wrong Tom to write it.

The following Sunday morning, an elderly maid cleaning the Pennsylvania State House told Clancy and Death, "I swears I seen Rafe Naider with me own eyes. He was flanked by two scowlin' men – though one sounded like a woman ta me – wearin' all black. Congress didn't wants 'm as he weren't properly voted inta office. 'ow could a true sober Christian man like Naider ever be elected? Do yous knows 'ow much rum and spirits them politicians 'as to buy ta bribes men to shows up? Them congressmen also throws out this man – *Tom*, Naider calls 'm–"

"Jefferson?" Clancy inquired.

"Twitchy man, clothes all disheveled–"

"Paine," Clancy and Death said in chorus.

"Outside the hall, Naider keeps talkin' 'bout justice and 'ow he wants Tom ta get on it, but not to do no more writin'. Naider says ta Tom if he could stands makin' corsets fer fussy women, sure he could repair sails that did nots complain."

"Aye, that was Naider," Clancy said to Death.

"This Tom gets insulted and he storms off."

"Where does – *did* Naider go?" Clancy asked.

"I donts know."

"You didn't follow him?"

"I 'ads ta finish cleanin'! Look at what pigs them congressmen is!" the old maid snapped, picking crumbled papers off the floor.

Death gave the maid a coin and one of his sweet smiles. "If you would be so kind, madam, have you heard any news of Roderick Redbeard or his house on the Delaware?"

"Yous goin' to kill him?"

"That is our intention, madam."

"'bout time someones did. Sorry, dears. Aparts from this job, I stays away from crooks 'n thieves the best I cans. 'ere, looks at what those mean, mean congressmen cuts out – the best part! Bit overwritten, but…"

The old maid pulled folded papers from her pocket and handed them to Clancy. Death gave her another coin and a kiss, and he and Clancy went to borrow John Dunlap's printing press while Dunlap was in church. Clancy and Death made a small fortune selling their own limited edition of the Declaration, deleting the hypocritical paragraph about "merciless Indian Savages," and reinstating Jefferson's mention of slavery from his original draft (expunged by Congress at South Carolina and Georgia's insistence). They trimmed Jefferson's 168-word paragraph haranguing the king to a pithy *He*

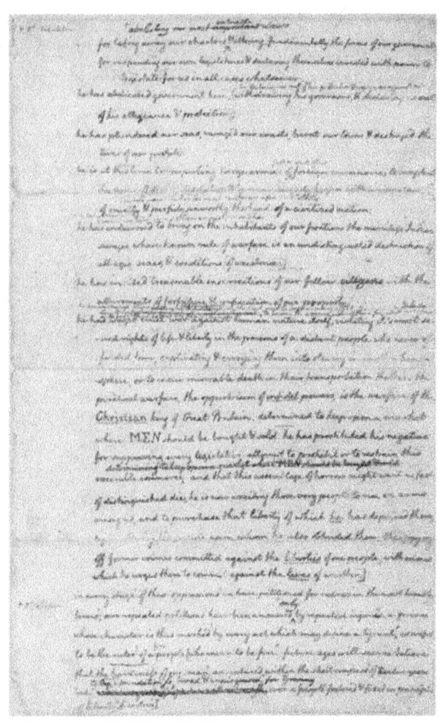

has failed to abolish slavery. Dr. Franklin and the old maid would be proud. They used the proceeds to buy stockings for Washington's army, a horse and wagon to tote their future arsenal, and Clancy sent money to Voltaire and the poor serfs of Saint-Claude. It was vital to keep good relations with the French; America would never win the war without their navy…and she really needed some restaurants.

Roderick's house on the Delaware was so well-guarded, Clancy and Death were unable to get within two miles of it. They wasted months trying to make friends at the taverns encircling Roderick's estate, hoping to learn of some weakness in Roderick's defenses. But no one was talking.

Apart from issuing the Declaration, Congress was useless. Getting funds to build up arms was taking far too long. These lawyers seemed to think their rhetorical hot air would magically blow British ships back to England. Clancy and Death grew downcast. How could they, two failing and flailing pirates, defeat the entire Royal Navy?

XIX
KISS A PIRATE

Their *Kiss-A-Pirate* scheme began as a joke. Death said if a woman like Margaret Gage was so overwhelmed by Clancy's sloppy kiss, how much money would an ordinary woman pay for a romantic kiss with a clean-shaven, better-looking younger man…like himself? Plenty, as it turned out, and it proved their most lucrative venture. They initially accepted gifts, but how many embroidered kerchiefs did a man need? They had to put their new boots down and tell their customers they would only accept coins, or their husbands' firearms.

Kissing was better than coitus, from a fundraising

standpoint. More women were willing to go that far. They had a special *Under-12-Half-Price!* day that was immensely popular, and almost all the little girls preferred Death. Truth be told, most of the Over-12s preferred Death. He was safer. Clancy and his French tongue virtuosity made women go home and rethink their lives. He was responsible for unraveling more marriages than he could possibly imagine.

The pirates soon grew tired of being treated like women. Most of their clients grabbed them by the napes of their necks, as though they were cats, and really tried to get their money's worth, digging their nails in, grinding their front teeth against theirs… Death was particularly irritated by the constant groping, though Clancy encouraged it, for it afforded him the opportunity to lift petticoats and steal pockets, killing two birds with one grope.

After months of trying to find some weakness in Roderick's defenses around his Delaware River estate, overnight, his guards vanished. Clancy and Death walked the grounds and found only smoking ruins and skeletal remains in the slave quarters. One elderly slave hiding in the woods came out when he recognized Clancy from an old portrait kept in a corner of the now-burned attic.

"Master Roderick left last night with some soldiers. *Burned to the ground by traitors to the Crown*, says he. Burned by Master Roderick, who pocketed the insurance money, says I."

Something caught Clancy's eye, and he went to investigate. Death handed the elderly slave all the coins he had and gave him the address of some people in Germantown who would help him.

Hanging from a tree by a tiny noose was one of Delia's Captain Death dolls. An *R* was drawn on the cheek. The eyes were ripped out. The doll's breeches were torn off, and its genital area burned.

Clancy dug a hole with his foot and quickly buried the doll before Death could see.

Death walked up to Clancy. "Let's go to Roderick's house

in Baltimore and blow it up."

"Roderick will stay close to General Washington," said Clancy. "My brother so loves being in for the kill."

"New York? An island! Surrounded by the sea!" Death chirped, skipping north.

They walked away from the ruins. Clancy wrapped his arm around Death.

"Stay close to me, William."

It was the first time Clancy had ever called him that. As proud he was of his name, constantly being called Death was dispiriting. No wonder no one wanted to be his friend. Sometimes he thought he might as well change his name to Bubonic Plague, or Syphilis.

William smiled. "I will. I promise…Clancy. *Red warrior.* Clancy of Culloden."

And to the Place of Darkness they went.

Things only got worse for General Washington after the disastrous Battle of Long Island. On October ninth, British warships *PHOENIX* and *ROEBUCK* (both with forty-four guns) and the frigate *TARTAR* (twenty guns) easily navigated over the American's ineffective chevaux de fries, sailed up the Hudson past Fort Washington and Fort

Lee, and anchored at Tappan Zee.

Did Washington learn his lesson and build better defenses for the river? No, the general's pride demanded the army spend valuable resources defending his namesake, Fort Washington – never mind the British were taking over the Hudson by the minute, stopping desperately needed supplies and chocolate from reaching Mount Constitution, recently re-named Fort Lee: "For Charles Lee? *He* was the best person they could think of?" Clancy barked. "Better to name it for one of his dogs – at least they're loyal." Clancy wrote to Gilbert du Motier, le marquis de la Fayette. The ambitious eighteen-year-old aristocrat's regiment recently disbanded, and Clancy informed the unemployed marquis that if he wanted fun, adventure and glory, go to Benjamin Franklin, the new Commissioner to France who would arrive in Paris soon, and then to America, even if it meant buying his own ship – and to bring his inheritance with him: "*Dépêche toi, mon cher marquis!*"

Rumors about Rafe Naider abounded: Naider had sailed to Florida and taken up with a sixteen-year-old girl and they were expecting their first child! Naider was the one who started the Great Fire in New York City! Naider was the one who betrayed Nathan Hale! Naider was killed by Indians, but his mother had assumed command of *JUSTICE* (or was it his sister?)! Naider was branded by the Sons of Liberty! (Bostonians frequently got Naider and Captain Death confused, to the annoyance of both men.) The most ludicrous rumor, and most believed, was that Naider had gone over to the British – he was a traitor! He spoiled everything! He just wanted his name in the gazettes! He was just *pretending* all these years to be working for the people…!

A t a Loyalist's party in New Jersey, Clancy liberated the dining room of its silverware and candlesticks while, in the library, Death laughed and flirted with a tall, slender lady. Death touched the fabric of her red gown. The lady blushed and cooled herself with a silk fan from Paris.

At the gunsmith's the next morning, the red gown entered, worn by Death. He had also procured the lady's wig and concealed the scar on his cheek with the silk fan from Paris.

"What a lovely daughter you have!" the gunsmith told Clancy, and proudly showed Death a fine rifle. Death ran a white-gloved finger along the barrel, and as he batted his beautiful long eyelashes at the guard, Clancy relieved the gunsmith of seven muskets.

n an alley near the Fraunces Tavern, their last *Kiss-a-Pirate* customer of the day asked Clancy if he was related to that Roderick Redbeard to whom her husband had sold a Franklin Rod, the finishing touch for that grand Tudor house overlooking the Hudson? Roderick had indeed sold the house – to his own slave transport company. Clancy cursed himself, but, amazingly, Death didn't berate him for not making further inquiries into who bought Father's old estate; he just smiled sadly and shrugged. Death was getting soft in his approaching middle age.

Clancy told the woman why yes, he was Roderick's "baby brother" (Clancy snickered to himself, knowing the phrase drove Roderick out of his skull with rage). The woman asked if Clancy would be so kind as to remind Roderick that he hadn't paid her husband for the Franklin Rod? Clancy paid her the money owed, and asked if she would do him a great favor and tell everyone she knew – especially her most talkative friends and milliners and wigmakers – that today she saw Captains Death and Redbeard depart on a ship bound for –

"On a coach!" interjected Death, who whispered to his idiot friend Clancy, "Are you trying to get innocent people killed? Roderick will sink every ship to get to me."

"Get to *you?*" Clancy whispered back. And where was Death's *thank you* for giving him top billing? But this was no time for self-importance. Clancy turned back to the woman –

"–a *coach* to Philadelphia, and the coachman told you they were heading to Florida for the winter. Then we can make our visit to my brother a big surprise." The woman promised, and

Clancy her one of his winks and a free kiss.

So, Roderick had made improvements to Father's old house. He would command the Hudson River and have America in a vise before Congress could agree on whether or not to wallpaper their chambers. To stop Roderick, pistols and rifles wouldn't do.

At the arsenal, the guard preferred Rubenesque women, and was not easily distracted by Death in the red gown. Hearing a leaf rustle, the guard turned and saw Clancy dragging an eighteen-pound gun out the gate, with the help of a handsome red ox he had borrowed from a farmer. With a strategic blow of his fan, Death knocked the guard out cold, hiked up his petticoats and, with the help of a white draft horse named Daisy, relieved the arsenal of a twelve-pound gun.

Clancy said it was time to retire the gown – preferably by burning it so no desperately poor woman would don it and attract the wrong sort of men (like themselves) – but Death wanted to flounce about one last time before they engaged a vessel and died in battle. *Very well,* Clancy sighed, and he took Death to the most expensive coffeehouse in New York, where Death had a scone, a biscuit, a huge slice of cake, and two cups of chocolate. With every bite and belch, a pin holding his gown together popped off and flew across the room.

To remind Clancy of what he wanted for his upcoming landmark birthday, Death had placed a large ship ornament in his powdered wig and pointed to it at every opportunity. Clancy decided to out-do Death and dressed as a macaroni in an even more ridiculous ceiling-high powdered wig, candy-colored silk clothes, and not one but three glued-on beauty spots. Death was not amused. They were so convincing as an unhappy couple that no one paid them the slightest attention, enabling them to reach into the pockets of every man unnoticed.

Clancy showed Death the front page of the *New York Tory Gazette: General Washington Abandons His Namesake, Forced to Retreat to Fort Lee,* and below, *Rafe Naider Wanted for Sedition,*

Sighted Near Poughkeepsie. With all the propaganda floating around, Clancy doubted validity of the first article, but he believed the second.

"Poughkeepsie it is," smiled Clancy.

Poughkeepsie?! They had been on dry land for twenty-two months, and Death was becoming land sick. Death's voice sank into its baritone range: "You said we were going to sea!"

Every customer in the coffeehouse turned and stared at Death. Death crescendoed into a higher pitch.

"You lying bastard! You promised!"

Clancy gently patted Death's clenched fist. "Now, now, the Hudson River is just as majestic as the Atlantic, my dear, and we shall stop and visit my brother's house. With your personality, I'm sure you will set it alight."

Clancy and Death exchanged piratical grins.

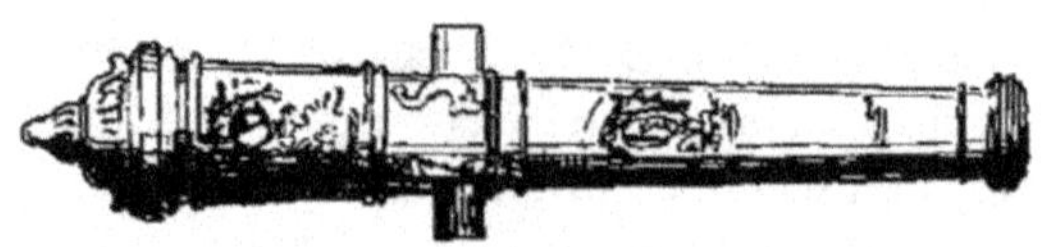

XX
THE TERRIBLE II

Clancy and Death hurried north, hoping to rendezvous with *JUSTICE* as she sailed south down the Hudson River to return to the Atlantic. That night in the village of Sleepy Hollow, an innkeeper told Clancy and Death that Rafe Naider was sighted a week earlier near pirate Captain Dobbs' ferry, five miles to the south.

The next morning, five Continental Army deserters told Clancy they saw Naider two days previously at Newburgh, thirty-five miles to the north. It was out of character for Naider to stay for so long and so far up any river. Clancy knew it was not *PHOENIX, ROEBUCK,* and *TARTAR* that were preventing Naider from sailing out to sea – it was Roderick.

As Clancy and Death drove their cannon north along the east bank of the Hudson, they stopped every ten minutes to look for *JUSTICE*...or *JUSTINE*...or *EJITS*. Near Cold Spring and Constitution Island, they spotted a ship anchored at the dock of a torched estate. After having part of her stern shot off by Roderick's guns, *JUSTINE* was now *JUST*.

aider wasn't surprised to see Clancy Redbeard lowering an eighteen-pound cannon onto his deck, but he swore he saw William Death riding the cannon. It couldn't be. This young man wore an unadorned dark coat. William was incapable of dressing so plainly.

Areebah and Kelvin's jaws dropped. Clancy dropped his swag bag at Naider's feet, twenty gold watches on Naider's desk, and sat on the gun, christened *Sarah's Revenge*.

Clancy grinned, "I tripped over several rich people."

"Permission to come aboard denied." Naider pointed to *Sarah's Revenge*. "Remove that."

"Your brother has guns," Kelvin said.

"From your rechristened ship, I guessed that," Clancy said. "How many?"

"Three."

"That's all?" Clancy grinned at Death. "This is going to be a piece of cake!"

Clancy unfurled the new plans of his father's estate. He had procured them from a builder Roderick had cheated, in exchange for Clancy's promise to kill Roderick. "Wonderful flaws in defense. My young friend and I take a barge. We disembark, slip into my brother's bedchamber, and kill him. Whilst my brother's sentries are busy killing us, *JUSTICE* – sorry, *JUST* – goes on her merry way, and you can sail to Philadelphia and sue whomever you like."

"I will not allow you and your young friend to commit suicide," said Naider. "I admire your courage, no matter how foolhardy it may be, but I was put on this earth to protect men like you from the consequences of their own folly. There is no need for bravado. This is a simple legal matter." Naider again pointed at the gun. "Areebah, remove that."

"It's just for show, Dad. We don't have any cannonballs," Areebah said as Kelvin carried a cannonball onboard, and Areebah went to fetch more. Death handed grateful Raiders five muskets, powder and shot. Clancy handed Naider the *New York Tory* clipping.

"SEDITION?" Naider gaped.

"Enjoy fighting that charge," Clancy said. "I'm sure after they hang you, there will be many angry letters to gazette editors. They'll write songs about you. In two hundred years, perhaps, a sainthood!"

"Go and speak to your brother," Naider said. "Make him see reason."

"The brother who killed my wife, had me tortured, and put this death sentence on you?"

Clancy turned and marched past Kelvin, who would have given him a Masonic salute if not for the three cannonballs he was hiding under his shirt.

As Clancy disembarked, Areebah grabbed him by his sword belt and pulled him until they were loin-to-loin.

"I'll be dead in a few hours," said Clancy.

"Words every woman longs to hear."

Areebah kissed him passionately and stuck her hand down his breeches. She quickly pulled her hand out. Clancy grimaced, reached down, and pulled out Areebah's muff pistol. It was smaller than his hand.

"Is this a metaphor?"

Areebah winked and climbed aboard *JUST.*

Naider realized that Clancy's young friend was indeed William Death. Naider said, "Did you have to advertise that it was you who sank Roderick's slave ship? That pride will be the death of you. William, stay here."

"I must help my friend."

"I think your friend took Dr. Franklin's electrical 'cure' one time too many."

As he bowed, two of Death's buttons popped off his breeches.

Naider grinned and wagged. *"To lengthen thy life, lessen thy meals."* And Death again remembered why he never re-joined Naider's Raiders. Who wants to sail with the world's biggest nag?

"Eat to please yourself, but dress to please others," Death sniffed at Naider's unfashionable coat with the wide cuffs from the '50s. Death picked up his buttons and disembarked.

Naider hurled another Franklinism: "*When in doubt, don't!*"

"*He that lives upon hope will die fasting,*" Death shot back.

"Fasting might help you fit in your breeches, William. *Never confuse motion with action.*"

"*When you're finished changing, you're finished.*"

On the dock, Death watched Clancy paint *Hello Brother* on their twelve-pound cannon. "Clancy, Naider is never, never in a million years, going to fire that gun."

"That's why it's coming with us," Clancy said.

From a neighbor, Clancy purchased a barge with just enough room for two pirates and a twelve-pound cannon, and docked her alongside *JUST*. While Naider was busy arguing with Kelvin and Areebah over *Sarah's Revenge*, sympathetic Raiders snuck the pirates a grappling hook, an oil lamp, and a fine rifle, though, in typical Raider thriftiness and/or disorganization, they had only acquired one bullet. Two girls from the village brought the pirates a pie, and a main course on a silver platter. Death kissed their cheeks and took the food. They asked if they might have a lock of his hair as a memento: the shops were clean out of Captain Death dolls. Clancy told Death to cut off that irritating forelock that kept blinding him. Death huffed and cut two small pieces from the back of his head. His fans squealed and ran to tell their friends. Death worked fast so they could cast off before the girls' friends came souvenir-hunting and left him tonsured.

Death secured *Hello Brother* and covered it with canvas. Clancy picked up the barge pole and pushed away from the dock. Death threw a kiss to Naider, who stood at the battered stern of *JUST*, watching Clancy and Death drift downriver on their vessel sporting a wooden sign: *TERRIBLE II.*

"William Death," Naider called. "You owe me fifty pounds!"

Death put his thumbnail between his front teeth and flicked Naider off.

Rafe Naider called, "Don't get hurt!"

Death maneuvered the barge close to the east shore while Clancy studied the plans of Roderick's house. Death saw something in the distance. Clancy grabbed the grappling hook and threw it around a tree, anchoring the barge.

Clancy looked through his spyglass at his brother's – once their father's – house: a huge Tudor mansion, fortified by a stone wall, with guns aimed at the river...

Seven thirty-two-pound guns.

"Piece of cake?" Death snarled.

"Kelvin never could count." Clancy drew up new plans. "We let the barge drift past the house, and while they're wondering what the hell it is...will it buy us enough time to get into the house? If we go at breakfast, there's no chance they won't see the barge...but if we go now, while the sun is in their eyes...my God...oh my God...his secretary...! We must kill him, too; he'll go after my children, and Mary, and Aunt Anne, and massacre the whole tribe..."

"Leave him to me," said Death.

"And his arsenal! We can inflict enough damage to buy General Washington time...but those guns! Naider is never going to get past them–" Clancy could barely breathe. His heart pounded. His brain was in a fog. "William...I can't think. I don't know how we...."

Death put his hand on Clancy's back. "I trust you, Clancy."

Clancy's breath returned. He kept thinking.

At twilight, Death soaked his blistered feet in the Hudson. Those narrow pointy slippers...how did women stand the pain? No wonder they were always in such a bad mood.

Death, breeches fixed and passing muster, ate the entire chocolate pecan pie straight out of the dish while Clancy studied his new diagram of the fortress.

Clancy lifted the top off the silver platter given to them by their admirers, made sure the small roasted chicken had not gone off, and pushed the platter over to Death.

"This is the last meal I shall ever have. I'm having pie." Death tossed his fork overboard. "And I'm not using a fork."

"Barbarian."

A flash of light came from the south. Clancy and Death turned and looked at the fortress.

Candle glow in a room overlooking the water.

Another flash, from above. They looked up.

Lightning.

"God," said Death in awe.

"An electrical discharge," said Clancy. "*When electrified clouds pass over, spires and lofty towers, trees and masts of ships draw the electrical fire and the whole cloud discharges there.*"

"God," said Death. "Lighting our way."

Clancy and Death exchanged piratical grins. They ripped the canvas off the cannon.

XXI
CAPTAIN DEATH

According to *Poor Richard's Almanack*, there was a full moon, but it was nowhere in sight. In pitch-blackness, the *TERRIBLE II* came within range of Roderick's guns. When lightning flashed, it reflected off Death's white shirt.

"William, put your coat on," Clancy whispered. "They'll see you."

"If they see me, they won't see you."

Clancy made sure their oil lamp stayed hidden behind the

cannon christened *Hello Brother*. They drifted past Roderick's first gun, and approached Roderick's dining room, aglow with candlelight. Clancy silently dropped anchor, moved the cannon into position, and lit slow match with the oil lamp. Death picked up a cannonball and went to drop it into the muzzle…

…and the ball wouldn't fit. Death tried again, and again, making a louder and louder *CLUNK! CLUNK!* with each futile attempt to shove the ball in.

"Naider took our balls," Death hissed in the dark. "I hate lawyers!"

"Did you do a test load?" Clancy hissed back. "No, you were too busy kissing women and getting drunk on pie!"

Clancy heard a loud *THUMP!* and *CRACK!* as though Death had dropped or thrown the cannonball down and split the barge's deck. When lightning flashed, Clancy saw Death doubled over in agony, clutching his chest.

"William?"

Had he been shot? A heart attack? God, no –

"William!"

Death let out the loudest belch in recorded history; so loud, two sentries on the fortress's top level, high above the water, were startled by the echo reverberating off the stone wall.

While Clancy banged his head on the cannon in frustration, Death shoved something down *Hello Brother's* barrel.

"Abandon ship!" Clancy ordered. "They have our position!"

"Ram! Ram!"

Clancy handed Death the ramrod. Ram *what?*

Death whispered, "The south wall!"

Clancy aimed the cannon and lit the fuse. The cannon fired, and they watched the beige projectile hurtle towards the large window.

In the dining room, Roderick and his secretary sat at a long table eating soup.

The large panoramic window shattered. Death's beige projectile ricocheted off the south wall and landed neatly in the middle of the table where the main course would soon be placed.

Roderick and his secretary stared at the roasted chicken.

Their minds spun. From the trajectory, the bird had to come from the middle of the Hudson –

A voice clucking *Bock bock bock!* came from the middle of the Hudson.

Roderick and his secretary went to the shattered window. Lightning flashed, and for a second, they thought they saw Captain Death standing on a cannon, waving to them.

In the dark, the voice from the middle of the Hudson called out:

"I'm sorry…did I scare you to *death*?"

Death grabbed the oil lamp and smashed it on the floor of the barge. The oil caught fire, creating footlights. Death raised a black flag: a crossed bones square and compasses, the skull with missing teeth and, above the skull, a *C*, all encircled by the motto *Virtus Junxit Mors Non Separabit*. The wind reversed direction, and the flag flew majestically.

Death picked up the rifle and aimed at Roderick.

Death fired.

Roderick and his secretary remained standing.

Clancy couldn't believe it. Death had missed.

Missed.

MISSED?!?! Clancy looked at Death, who, forelock covering his eyes, looked like a raven-haired sheepdog.

"You vain peacock," Clancy said. "You preening, narcissistic–"

But this was no time for reprimands. Clancy grabbed a spool of wire. He stuck a torch in the flames and waved it.

"Oh, Ro-der-ick! It's your baby brother, Clancy!"

As Death brushed his hair out of his eyes, Roderick stuck his head out the shattered window and yelled upwards at his sentries:

"FIRE! FIRE!"

Death ducked behind *Hello Brother* as a lobby of fire from the sentries on the top level peppered the burning barge.

A ball from Roderick's fifth cannon hit the front of the barge. Death fell backwards, hitting his head on *Hello Brother.*

Seeing stars and partly blinded by his hair, Death looked for his friend.

"Clancy? Clancy!"

Clancy had vanished.

n cannon room four, the gunners were so engrossed in their card game they didn't notice the little skirmish on the river. Dripping wet, Clancy crawled through the cannon port and over the thirty-two-pound gun.

"Cards! I wish you had called me," said Clancy, walking past the stack of cannonballs to the door.

The door flung open, hitting Clancy in the nose and knocking him back against the wall. Roderick's secretary charged in.

"You'll all hang for this! FIRE!"

While the secretary kicked a gunner, Clancy eased himself from behind the door, snuck out, and ran to cannon room five, where three middle-aged gunners were prepping for a second shot.

"Run for your lives!" Clancy shouted. "It's William Death!"

"Captain Death?"

The three gunners ran out of cannon room five, knocking Clancy over as they fled down the corridor. Clancy picked himself up and opened the door to cannon room six. Three gunners were preparing hotshot.

"Run for your lives!" Clancy shouted. "It's Captain Death!"

The seventeen-year-old gunners stared at Clancy.

Finally, one of them asked, "Who?"

"Who? WHO?"

Teenagers! Did they ever read gazettes? Clancy considered brandishing Areebah's muff pistol, but it was so embarrassingly small, and had no ammunition… Clancy ran out, and headed to cannon room three.

O n the burning barge, Death loaded his rifle with triangular pieces of eight, the only ammunition he could find.

Roderick's sentries reloaded. In cannon room four, Roderick's secretary aimed the gun at Death.

Death fired. One of the pieces hit a gunner in the eye, another in the nose, a third imbedded itself in the secretary's wig.

"*Bock bock bock!*" Death clucked. Then he saw the secretary aiming the cannon at him, and he ducked behind *Hello Brother*.

Death heard a loud splash behind him. Death looked but saw nothing.

Roderick screamed, "FIRE!"

An object whizzed from behind Death and hit the muzzle of cannon four, knocking it out of position as the secretary fired it. Cannon four's ball hit the water just a few feet short of Death.

A horn sounded *Naider's Call*. The dark clouds parted, and the full moon illuminated *JUST – JUSTICE* – anchored behind the barge. Kelvin sponged *Sarah's Revenge*; Areebah lined up the next shot. She was under orders not to kill or maim Roderick, only to "make him take notice," so she aimed at cannon room two.

"That's what you get when you fire spitballs," Kelvin snarled at Areebah.

"Try to take the right balls next time!"

Naider stood by the mainmast eating popcorn, taking a rare break from work to watch the spectacle of pirates taking on Roderick. "Don't hurt anyone!" he reminded his Raiders between bites.

"KILL NAIDER!" shouted Roderick. "FIRE!"

The sentry aiming at Death turned and, attempting to shoot Naider, instead hit the barrel of the sentry's gun on his right.

Five of Naider's Raiders fired muskets, aiming above the sentries' heads.

Clancy entered cannon room three, directly below Roderick's dining room window. The gunners were aiming at Death. Clancy whistled. The gunners spun around.

"Let me show you lads some fun! Let's just push this back a bit..."

The eager young gunners, who hadn't had a moment's fun since Roderick impressed them into his service, happily helped Clancy push the cannon back, and pointed the muzzle at the wall next to the cannon port.

"Make ready!" Clancy smiled.

The gunners fired, and the cannonball blasted through the wall next to the cannon port, making a nice big hole.

"That's grand," Clancy complimented them. "Want to have even more fun? One, two, three!"

Clancy and the gunners pushed the cannon through the hole, and it crashed down onto the rocks on the shore.

Areebah fired *Sarah's Revenge*. The cannonball went straight into the barrel of cannon number two, the force of the ball knocking the cannon to the back of the room.

Then, silence. In the dark, Naider heard Roderick's voice:

"Make ready!"

Lightning flashed and Naider and his Raiders saw three of Roderick's cannon aiming at *JUSTICE*.

Naider, in his understated way, said, "Oh, oh."

Kelvin and Areebah grabbed Naider's arms and dragged him towards the bow.

"Fire!" Roderick yelled.

Cannon three blew off *JUSTICE's* rudder. Cannon six fired hotshot and set *JUSTICE's* rigging and masts on fire. Cannon one hit *JUSTICE's* hull at the water line near the bow. Areebah's arm was blown off, as was Kelvin's right ear. *Sarah's Revenge* rolled off the deck and plunged into the river.

Bock bock bock...

Roderick looked down and saw Death, on the rocks below,

waving to him. Death drew his rapier and charged into the blown-out wall of cannon room three.

n the fortress corridor, cheerful Clancy skipped past eight of Roderick's older guards, who recognized him, but couldn't quite believe it.

"Good evening!" Clancy smiled at them. "My, such wonderful bearing you all have!"

They smiled back, chortling as they recalled the stories of the stupid, inept Bastard of Redbeard. Clancy went to the powder room.

USTICE began to sink. Raiders jumped ship and swam west bank of the Hudson.

Roderick continued commanding from the dining room, chicken drumstick in hand.

"Reload!"

Roderick heard screams. He looked down. Four gunners, covered in blood, fell out of the blasted-out hole in cannon room three.

Roderick's secretary ran down the corridor past Clancy, who was absorbed in picking the powder room lock. The secretary kept running, until he realized who and what he saw. Clancy pointed Areebah's pistol at him. The secretary took a step back, but when he squinted and saw that the muff pistol was so tiny that a shot to his forehead would barely inflict a minor headache, he charged. With his other hand, Clancy aimed at the secretary. Knowing Clancy's ambidexterity, the secretary stopped and ducked – and then realized Clancy was only pointing his index finger at him, his thumb raised like a cock. The secretary charged. Clancy unlocked the door, ran into the powder room and slammed the door in the secretary's face.

The secretary pushed back his bruised wig, picked out one of Death's pieces of eight, and knocked on the door.

"Oh, Clancy!"

"Whoooooooo is it?"

"Please come out Clancy."

"Uh, it's awfully loud out there. I think I'll just stay in here and read. Why aren't there any magazines in the magazine?"

Death came down the corridor. He had used the river water to slick his hair back. Now, nothing obscured his vision. Death stuck his rapier under his blood-soaked shirt and ripped it off.

"I want my piece of eight back."

"So you can buy some little boy's flesh?" The secretary pocketed Death's money and removed his wig.

Death recognized the secretary…and took two steps back.

The secretary walked towards Death. "I remember you," said the secretary, no longer concealing his French accent. "You were the boy on the *TERRIBLE*. We let you live. And this is how you thank us." The secretary drew his sword. "But you are no Captain Death."

The secretary lunged, and Death ran the secretary through the neck. Death reached into the secretary's pocket, took his piece of eight back, and pulled his blade out of the secretary's neck. The secretary fell back, and Death walked over the secretary as though he were a rug.

The three guards watching from the end of the corridor turned and ran up the stairs.

Death went to the powder room door.

"Clancy!"

In the powder room, Clancy stuck his hand through a small window near the top of the wall, straining to grab something that lay outside just out of reach. "William, get out! Get out!"

"I have to attend to your brother."

"Get out! Please, get out!"

Death went up the spiral staircase, clucking *bock bock bock…*

On the second level, Roderick and three guards heard a chicken clucking. At the end of the darkened corridor, sparks flew as a rapier blade scraped against the stone walls and ceiling.

"*Bock bock bock!*"

Captain Death stepped into the torchlight. A guard charged Death. Death grabbed the guard's blade, pushed him back with his foot, flipped the sword and stabbed the guard in the chest. The second guard charged like a maniac. Death waited until the guard was almost on him. Death dropped down and let the guard run onto his rapier.

The third guard, a wiser man in his forties, approached, his sword sheathed. He held up a small purse.

"I apologize for any inconvenience my present position may have caused you, Captain Death, and I hope you will accept this as a small token of apology for any thoughtless comment I may have made about you or your abilities while in a state of drunken jealousy…"

Death grabbed the purse, gave the guard a quick smile and a flick of his head, and the guard ran past him and down the corridor.

Death turned to Roderick.

Roderick lowered his sword, raised his pistol, and shot Death in the right shoulder.

Death knew Roderick was unsportsmanlike, but this was plain rude. Death dropped his rapier.

"O Death, where is thy victory? O Death, where is thy sting?" Roderick said as he sheathed his sword and unholstered his second pistol.

Death picked up his rapier, turned, and ran down the corridor. Roderick fired and hit Death in the right calf. Death dropped his beloved rapier and disappeared in the darkness. He fell down the staircase and hit the floor of the lower level.

Someone picked him up and carried him down the corridor to a medieval suit of armor on display, which held a lit torch in its hand. Death looked up, and saw it was Clancy who carried him. Clancy kicked the armor's shin. A hidden door in the wall opposite the armor popped opened. Death grabbed the torch. Clancy carried Death into the secret chamber and shut the door.

Roderick and two guards came down the staircase and ran down the corridor and past the hidden door.

 n the secret chamber, Clancy gently put Death down on the stone floor. Clancy stuck the torch in a wall sconce, took off his coat, and put it under Death's head. Clancy pulled off Death's boot and examined the entrance and exit wounds; the ball went clean through. Clancy tied his kerchief around Death's leg.

With his sgian-dubh, Clancy dug the ball out of Death's shoulder. Death did not cry out, but he could not stop his legs from kicking and flailing.

The ball made a tiny *plink!* on the stone floor when Clancy tossed it aside.

Clancy patted Death's cheek.

"Good boy."

Clancy took his coat and put it on Death, easing his right arm gently through the sleeve. Clancy made a sling out of his shirt and slipped Death's right arm into it. Clancy put Death's boot back on him, wrapped his arms around Death's waist, and helped him stand.

Death whimpered, "I dropped my sword."

Clancy unbuckled his sword belt and put it around Death's waist.

In the corridor, Roderick and his guards felt the walls, trying to find an opening.

Roderick saw the suit of armor. Knowing his father and his childish sense of humor, Roderick guessed there was a hidden chamber where the armor was "looking."

"Oh, Clancy!" Roderick called.

Clancy and Death's blood froze.

"Clancy, Clancy...I'm not angry with you," Roderick cooed as though talking to a five-year-old. "You found one of father's secret chambers."

Clancy sheathed his sgian-dubh and stuck it in Death's left boot.

Roderick purred, "Hand over William Death, and all will be forgiven."

Clancy felt the floor. He found the hidden wooden trap

door, painted like stone. Clancy pried it up and showed Death the escape passage.

"Go down the river to Fort Lee. We met upon the level, and we part upon the square."

"No, Clancy, you go."

Roderick shouted down the corridor, "Bring the cannon! Blow this wall down!"

Death said, "I will never leave you. At least we can die together...as brothers."

"Go, William."

"We will not see each other in heaven. I am not going there, because of what I am."

"What clergyman told you that?!" Clancy grabbed William by his coat and pulled him until they were nose-to-nose. "You are God's instrument on earth. Your work has just begun."

Clancy took off Death's gold Masonic ring and slipped it back onto Death's finger.

Death cried. "I've killed you. I was so vain, I didn't get a haircut. And I didn't test the cannon. You were right – I was too busy thinking about the pie."

Clancy cradled Death's face. "When I die, I will be smiling, thinking of you...and that chicken."

Clancy and Death exchanged one last piratical grin.

"I was right – you are not your father," Death said. "He would have handed me over."

Death winked at Clancy and jumped down the hole.

Clancy sang as he replaced the false stone, "*Farewell and adieu to you fair Irish ladies, for we've received orders to sail for Poughkeepsie...*"

In the corridor, Roderick looked at the suit of armor...

...and remembered. Roderick kicked the armor in the shin. The hidden door opened. Roderick and the guards ran into the chamber.

Clancy stood on the false stone.

Roderick asked, "Where is Captain Death?"

"Who?"

Roderick slapped Clancy across the face and turned to his

guards. "One of Father's escape passages is in here. It leads to the river!"

Two of the guards ran out, the other two restrained Clancy. Clancy looked around the chamber. "This is where Father used to hide his booty."

"You mean, his whores," Roderick corrected Clancy. "Like your mother."

"Father showed me this room on my fifth birthday," Clancy remembered. "That was the happiest day of my life, the day he told me I had a big brother named Roderick, who would always love me, and always look after me. And later that night, you tried to drown me in the bath."

"Bastard Clancy, on the authority granted me by the British Crown, I sentence you to death."

"Oh...may I please be hanged?" begged Clancy.

Roderick smiled. "As it was your mother's whoredom made my mother hang herself, I see the justice."

n the fortress courtyard, Roderick marched Clancy, hands tied behind his back, to prefabricated gallows.

"Father's reputation confused me," said Clancy. "One person would say he was a pirate, the next person said he was a prince. Mother called me a little murderer; Father called me a big coward. I didn't know what to do...so I did nothing. I did nothing with my life."

Death hid amongst the rocks at the foot of the fortress. *JUSTICE*, in flames, slowly sank. Naider and his Raiders had abandoned ship.

Death came out of the rocks and limped toward the river, when flashes of lightning illuminated everything – including him. Death ducked back into the rocks.

A sentry pointed out Death's position to the other sentries. They lined up and prepared to fire.

In the courtyard, Clancy saw the sentries taking aim. Clancy looked up at the sky. The moon peeked through the black clouds.

"Father did teach me a few useful things," Clancy said to Roderick. "How to pick a lock, how to slip a rope–"

Clancy lifted his free hands. The guards pointed their guns at him. Clancy took the rope from a young guard attempting to tie a noose. Clancy made a loop: "Here's the king's head. Now, strangle the king. Now, poke him in the eye." Clancy poked the rope through the loop, smiled at the guard, and put the knot around his own neck. He tossed the other end up and over the wooden beam.

Lightning flashed. A sentry spotted *JUSTICE's* ship's boat, with Kelvin and one-armed Areebah rowing Naider away from the burning brigantine.

"Rafe Naider, eleven o'clock!" the sentry shouted.

"Make ready!" Roderick yelled. The sentry repeated the order to the gunners below, and the six-remaining cannon, all loaded with hotshot, aimed at Naider.

"Did Father ever teach you his favorite trick?" Clancy asked Roderick, looking up at the brass lightning rod on the wooden house's apex. "What fun you can have, taking a Franklin Rod's grounding wire, and rigging it to some sort of explosive device..."

At long last, Roderick realized that Clancy was not as stupid as he had thought.

Clancy closed his eyes, finally, at peace.

"Oh, I did *something*."

A huge bolt of lightning struck the Franklin Rod. The electrical charge ran down the grounding wire, through a small window, and into the powder room, where Clancy had attached the wire to a keg of gunpowder and wired the keg to the other kegs of gunpowder in the room.

Death ran into the river and swam towards Naider's boat. As the sentries aimed at Death, the powder room blew up. Naider, Areebah, and Kelvin watched Roderick's fortress explode.

Flying debris hit Death in the back of the head and he went

under.

Cannon one and two tumbled down onto the rocks below. The walls above cannon three, four and five collapsed. The gunners manning cannon six and seven fled as the ceilings started cracking.

The black clouds parted, and the moon emerged.

At dawn on his thirty-fifth birthday, half-drowned William Death, holding Blackbeard's cutlass, clung to a piece of driftwood lodged against a fallen tree near the western shore. Disoriented from having lost so much blood, he thought he was still on the eastern shore, and in the cold water had pulled his way through fallen branches and trees a quarter mile in the wrong direction. Only when the current grew stronger did he realize he was heading north.

The current dislodged the driftwood, and Death was pulled away from the shore and down the river.

Death lost his grip on the driftwood and went under. Choking and coughing, still holding onto the cutlass, he flailed, trying to stay afloat with his one good arm. He went down. The tip of Blackbeard's cutlass poked up from the depths.

A gloved hand grabbed the sword's blade and pulled Death up. Someone else grabbed Death by his coat collar and pulled him out of the water.

Death came to his senses and found himself in a boat, wrapped in a blanket. He looked up at his rescuer, a nervous man in his thirties, papers sticking out of his coat, fingers black with ink stains. It was the sickly twitchy big-nosed writer he saw on the *LONDON PACKET*.

When Death saw the man commanding the boat, he thought it was Clancy – a tall, greying redhead, but his hair was neatly in a queue, he was clean-shaven and had the perpetually frozen face of a stoic....

General Washington did not recognize William Death. He had never seen the young man without Clancy Redbeard by his side.

At Washington's side was William Lee. Mr. Lee cleared his throat and whispered, "General. His ring..."

Washington saw that Death wore Clancy's Masonic ring. And when he saw Roderick's smoldering fortress, Washington knew that Clancy Redbeard had, at last, done something.

The rising sun was suddenly blocked. Washington, Death and Tom Paine looked up. A sixteen-gun brig, *NEW YORK*, sailed past them, flying a yellow flag with a coiled rattlesnake and the motto *Don't Tread on Me*. The brig sailed downriver to Roderick's fortress, now a smoking pile of rubble, the sun shining just above the ruins. The brig fired at the last standing sections of the wall, above cannon six and seven. She knocked them down, burying Roderick's two remaining guns under stone.

The *NEW YORK* turned to starboard and fired at forty-four-gun *PHOENIX* and *ROEBUCK*, and twenty-gun *TARTAR*, hitting all three, causing minor damage. The British ships, taken by surprise, just sat there, their stunned officers staring at the upstart *NEW YORK*.

The American brig circled the wreck of Rafe Naider's ship. The Franklin Rod on the brigantine's mainmast refused to go under, as did *JUSTICE's* stern, poking out of the water as though mooning her assailants. Only two characters of her former name remained: *US*.

THE END

Many Thanks

Portsmouth Historic Dockyard, Rijksmuseum Amsterdam, Het Scheepvaartmuseum Amsterdam, National Maritime Museum Greenwich, Mystic Seaport Connecticut, New Bedford Whaling Museum, Boston Tea Party Museum, Maritime Museum of San Diego, Mariners' Museum Norfolk, Musée national de la Marine Paris, New York Historical Society, Philadelphia Historical Society, Museum of the American Revolution Philadelphia, Independence National Historical Park, American Philosophical Society, Benjamin Franklin Museum Philadelphia, Benjamin Franklin House London, The Franklin Post Office, Mütter Museum of the College of Physicians of Philadelphia, John Adams National Historical Park Quincy Massachusetts, Papers of Thomas Jefferson Princeton University, National Park Service, University of Virginia, Project Gutenberg, Library of Congress, Archive.org, Wikipedia and its contributors who provided sources, the long-dead artists whose work appears in a context they never dreamed, British Library, Stephen Moore, Ron Carnegie, Dr. Edgar MacDonald, Nat Lasley, Barbara Swanson, Metropolitan Museum of Art, Museum of Fine Arts Boston, Philadelphia Museum of Art, Los Angeles County Museum of Art, National Portrait Gallery London, Colonial Williamsburg Foundation, Waterman's Museum Yorktown, Jamestown Settlement, Monticello, and Mount Vernon.

Wroughten Books logo Jean Leon Gerome Ferris, Library of Congress.

Title Page: Cannon, *Artillery Through the Ages: A Short Illustrated History of Cannon, Emphasizing Types Used in America* Author/Illustrator Albert Manucy, National Park Service

Map of Virginia Joshua Fry and Thomas Jefferson's Father Peter, Library of Congress

Blackbeard (aka Edward Teach)'s severed head, *The Pirates Own Book* by Charles Ellms, Illustrator Unknown

Capture of the Pirate, Blackbeard Jean Leon Gerome Ferris

Hanging of Captain Kidd *The Pirates Own Book*, Illustrator Unknown

O! the Fatal Stamp *Pennsylvania Journal and Weekly Advertiser*

The Grampus Orca (Killer Whale) J. Stewart. Sir William Jardine's *The Naturalist's Library* Vol. VI *Natural History of the Ordinary Cetacea Or Whales*

Justice Rechtvaardigheid, Hendrick Goltzius. Rijksmuseum Amsterdam

Silenus, a Satyr and a Goat Giorgio Ghisi, Los Angeles County Museum of Art

Stove designed by Benjamin Franklin

Willem van de Velde Sketching a Sea Battle Joseph Ignace van

Hoey, State Hermitage Museum, Russia

Blackbeard the Pirate, *A General History of the Lives and Adventures of the Most Famous Highwaymen, Murderers, Street-Robbers, &c* by Captain Charles Johnson, Illustrator unknown

George Washington Charles Willson Peale, Washington and Lee University

Armonica invented by Benjamin Franklin Illustrator unknown, Library of Congress

George Washington (and a model in London portraying William "Billy" Lee) John Trumbull, Metropolitan Museum of Art

An Incident in the Rebellion of 1745 (Battle of Culloden) Attributed to David Morier, Palace of Holyroodhouse, Edinburgh

Benjamin Franklin Drawing Electricity from the Sky by Benjamin West, Philadelphia Museum of Art

David Hume Allan Ramsay, Scottish National Gallery

Thomas Paine Auguste Millière after George Romney after William Sharp, National Portrait Gallery London

Sea Captains Carousing in Surinam John Greenwood, Saint Louis Art Museum

John Adams Artist unknown, after John Singleton Copley, National Park Service, Adams National Historical Park

Voltaire's *A Philosophical Dictionary* Frontispiece, Illustrator unknown. London: W. Dugdale

Join or Die attributed to Benjamin Franklin, Library of

Congress

Essai Sur L'Électrcité des Corps Frontispiece, Jean Antoine
Illustrator unknown

Anne Bonny, *Charles Johnson's Book of Pirates,* Illustrator
unknown

George III Johann Zoffany, The Royal Collection; book cover
styled after Al Franken's book *Rush Limbaugh is a Big Fat Idiot*

Paul Revere John Singleton Copley, Museum of Fine Arts
Boston

Mrs. Thomas Gage (Margaret Kemble Gage) John Singleton
Copley, Timken Museum of Art, San Diego

George Washington (and William Lee?) by Charles Willson
Peale, DeWitt Wallace Museum, Colonial Williamsburg
Foundation

Common Sense by An Englishman (that would be Thomas Paine).
Published by Robert Bell, Philadelphia

Declaration of Independence by John Trumbull, United States
Capitol

Thomas Jefferson's Draft of the Declaration of American
Independence, page 3, Library of Congress

U.S. Seal Pierre Eugène Du Simitière – rejected by Congress.
U.S. Department of State's pamphlet *The Great Seal of the
United States*

Captain Kidd in New York Harbor Jean Leon Gerome Ferris, Library of Congress

Forcing a Passage on the Hudson Dominic Serres the Elder

Beauty's Lot (Skull wearing wig) Published by William Humphrey, London. Library of Congress

Nearing the End P. Graham, A.R.A (Lightning at sea), *Macleod of Dare, A novel* by William Black, British Library

Author Motifs by Frank C. Papé from *Jürgen: A Comedy of Justice* by James Branch Cabell

"ILLUSTRATIONS" and Drop Cases *Alphabeta Et Characteres*, John Theodor and John Israel De Bry, Frankfurt

Additional Drop Cases *The Comical Hotch-Potch, or the Alphabet turn'd Posture Master* Printed for & sold by Carington Bowles

Book designed by the author

Jürgen Vsych (pronounced Yurgen VY-zick) was born in Hollywood and educated in Scotland. An independent filmmaker and former professional bagpiper, Vsych lives on a schooner, sailing the seven seas and the Mississippi, Delaware, Hudson, Thames, and Clyde.

TheCaptainDeath.com

9 780974 987941